Dead of Winter

An Anthology

Dead of Winter

An Anthology

Mighty Quill Books
Pittsburgh

Copyright © 2017 by Mighty Quill Books
Individual author copyrights © 2016 on all stories, except "Huntress of Bur" © 2015 Justin Chasteen.
Cover art © 2017 by A.M. Rycroft

Edited by Stacy Overby and Katherine Pekin

All rights reserved. This book or any portion thereof may not be reproduced or used in any manner whatsoever without the express written permission of the publisher except for the use of brief quotations in a book review or scholarly journal.

The "M" and quill design is a trademark of Mighty Quill Books, a subsidiary of Mighty, LLC.

First Printing: 2017

ISBN 978-0-9860884-8-3

Mighty Quill Books
www.mightyquillbooks.com

Special discounts are available on quantity purchases. For details, contact the publisher by email at info@mightyquillbooks.com or at the following address:

Mighty Quill Books
c/o Mighty, LLC.
370 Castle Shannon Blvd., 10366
Pittsburgh, PA 15234

We would like to give a special thanks to Juliet, Kat, Nina, Nikki, and Stacy for all your tireless work on this project. It wouldn't have turned out as good as it did without your help!

CONTENTS

Foreword - A.M. Rycroft - i

The Darkness Has Teeth - Pamela Jeffs - 1

The Huntress of Bur - Justin Chasteen - 15

Fry Machete's Monsters, Munchies, and Mayhem - Stuart Conover - 23

Only in Death - Zoey Xolton - 41

These Claws Dig Shallow Graves - Kevin Holton - 47

Slipped Stitch - KT Wagner - 59

Spotlight - David J. Gibbs - 67

Coyoteman - Robert Perret - 89

The Killers - Meredith Schindehette - 103

Annabel Lee - Erin J. Kahn - 121

About the Authors - 127

FOREWORD

A.M. Rycroft

Story rules are boring. I decided this after sifting through one themed open call after another, searching for a home for a couple of my horror shorts. Just about all of the submission guidelines included a theme for submitted stories.

Content guidelines are important, of course. Explicit sex and violence aren't appropriate for every publication. But, I started to wonder why so many publishers wanted to restrict entries to a specific theme. Why not really open things up and take whatever an author wanted to throw at them? That seems much more interesting to me.

So, when we at Mighty Quill Books decided to open up submissions for a dark fiction anthology, we decided at the start that even though the title would be *Dead of Winter*, it would be non-themed. We asked authors to keep explicit sex and outrageous violence/gore out of their pieces, but beyond that, it was a free for all. It just had to be dark fiction.

If you've never heard the term "dark fiction",

you might assume this means horror, when in fact, it means so much more than that. "Dark fiction" refers more to the mood of a given story than a specific plot type.

A dark fiction story can be horror, but it can also be fantasy, science fiction, thriller, or dystopian. It can be even more things than that, but I think you get the idea.

Fortunately, the mix of stories we received hit on many different facets of dark fiction, though there was plenty of horror to go around. Paring down the list to just the ten best felt, at times, like a monumental task, because there were just so many good entries.

No matter whether you are a horror fan, or you like a little fantasy, a little science fiction, or a little dystopian fiction, we think you're going to find stories to love in this anthology. We hope you'll let us know how we did, and that you'll look for more works from the authors in this anthology. They're all authors to look out for.

A.M. Rycroft
Publisher and Author
Mighty Quill Books

Dead of Winter

An Anthology

THE DARKNESS HAS TEETH

Pamela Jeffs

It's 11:30 p.m., if the watch on my wrist is working correctly. A full moon, burning orange, hangs low on the distant horizon. A ruined highway stretches out before me. As I walk my boots catch edges of broken bitumen, but I ignore the distraction. My mind is elsewhere. At midnight, I will have another chance to travel back through time—another chance to put things right. My fingers toy with the weapon concealed inside my pocket. The knot of tension in my chest is the size of a fist. I've failed so many times.

A derelict house emerges out of the night, two stories high. It clings to the side of the highway like a pale ghost. The roof is shattered, tiles fallen away to reveal broken trusses. Twin verandahs smile at me crookedly with their gap-toothed balustrades. The once ornate windows behind them are shadowed.

I pause at the bottom of the splintered staircase leading up to the first-story verandah. I scratch at my beard, looking up at the old wicker chairs lying tumbled about, broken and crumbling.

Dust covers everything. No footprints mar the even surface, but that means nothing. The things I fear don't always leave footprints.

Dust billows around my ankles as I take the four steps. Everything is quiet. I make my way to the door which, like the roof, is shattered. But this time, it's the embedded shotgun pellets in the doorframe that tell the story. Someone once made a final stand here.

I push my way past, splinters from door catching in the cuff of my jacket. I brush them away. I take a breath. I cross the threshold.

Inside, the foyer is dim. A fallen barricade of furniture spills out across the floor. My gaze sweeps the room.

More furniture.

An old ragged rug.

A male corpse, shotgun held in lax fingers.

The perfectly intact body lies fallen like a broken doll against a sofa. I shudder. I hate how bodies don't decompose anymore. Demon toxins. The poison preserves the flesh. And the affected lie where they fall. That is, until their bodies are needed again.

I step closer. Thin moonlight streaming in through a window reveals his features to me. White hair, wrinkled skin, and blue eyes staring sightlessly into the distance. He has the look of an old timer, possibly one of the original sugarcane

farmers who dwelt in these parts.
I take another step. The corpse doesn't move. A good sign. I see an old leather wallet sprawled open on the floor. The license reads John Everton. I wish I hadn't seen it. Knowing the man's name only adds to my burden of guilt. My mistakes are why old John is lying here dead.
I turn my attention back to the fallen barricade. The haphazard array of furniture lies across an open doorway that leads back further into the house. The rooms beyond it stand dark. I reach into my pack, pull out my torch and turn it on. Climbing over more wicker furniture, I push a small desk to one side and step through the doorway.
Beyond the opening is a hall. The floor, walls and chandeliers are layered thick with dust. I flick my torch over each surface, looking for the cracks I hope aren't there. The initial sweep reveals nothing, but any fissures could still be hidden.
I lift my boot and thud it hard against the floor. The old timbers groan in protest. Then slowly the dust covering the gaps between the boards begins to filter away.
There are cracks, all right. So many.
I slowly back out of the door, past the desk and over the wicker furniture. I try to do so quietly but the hard rubber soles of my boots scuff and each scrape sets my teeth on edge.

Then I hear it.

The sound of the demons.

The sound of their black tar bodies slithering out of the cracks and crawling over the floor.

I move fast. I'm back in the foyer. My breathing is shallow. I swing the light of my torch in a blue-white arc around the room. It passes over the couch, flicks past the window, washing out the spill of moonlight. It follows on, falling on the doorway leading outside to fresh air and freedom—and there in the opening stands John Everton's corpse, now animated, with shotgun loaded and ready.

I should never have come in here.

The corpse snarls at me. His teeth glitter yellow in the beam of my torch. His silver hair shines white and his eyes are now two orbs of darkness. I can see the demon behind them, the one that's taken up residence in his empty head. It's smiling. It's anticipating dinner. Me.

The cracked glass in the window shatters as I plough my shoulder into it. I slither out over the sill and land hard on the gravel below. I struggle to my feet and turn to run.

But I pull up short—halted by the business end of a double barrel shotgun aimed at my head.

John Everton's now black eye has me lined up in the gun sight. I stare straight back into it—that pool of midnight ink. From the corner of my own eye, I see his trigger finger twitch but, before he can pull it, a shrill electronic beeping sounds out. I glance down.

My watch.

It's midnight.

And with midnight comes the magic.

The electric crackle of the time portal forming makes my hair stand on end. A torrent of wind kicks up, blasting static dust into clouds. John Everton staggers backwards. His gun shifts to aim uselessly at the sky. Then the portal burgeons into life, a ring of blue fire engulfing me, drawing me down and drowning me in light.

***

I open my eyes and instinctively know I am fifteen years old. I am lying flat on a perfect green lawn, the sun shining down on me from above. Behind me is the house I just escaped from, but it is now well maintained. In the distance, fields full of gently waving sugarcane ripple in a soft, warm breeze. I reel. I forget how striking the world was before I ruined it.

I sit up and look down at my watch. I press the button on the side, setting the alarm. Fifteen minutes before the portal resets and I am sent back. Not long, but hopefully it's enough time. I get to my feet and reach into my pocket.

The weapon is not much to look at. It's a slender metal cylinder I made to be as thin and long as a pencil. Inside it, I have harnessed a spark of time taken from within the portal. The cylinder burns cold in my hand, the ember within heavy with the weight of history. This all began with a small fissure in a rock, a crack that I used time to force wider. A terrible mistake made almost thirty years ago.

I walk around the side of the house and follow the gravel path leading to the back. My thoughts hover, insistent, at the forefront of my mind. The mistake. I remember being twelve when it happened, too young to understand what using my mind to manipulate the flow of time would do. I didn't mean to widen the cracks of the world, didn't mean to stretch their fabric so thin as to create infinite doorways to a dimension of darkness. But the fact remains: I flooded the world with demons. Now all I want is to send the bastards back.

The gravel soon gives way to lush garden. The quiet trickling of water over rocks draws my attention. I dig through a hedge of gardenia bushes and find the small fountain and pond nestled at their center. Goldfish hang lazy in the water, long tails brushing at the water lily stems.

To one side of the pond, I see what I am looking for—a large granite boulder. Its mossy green back is dappled with sunlight, a small swallow sits on top of it flicking his head side to side as he searches for insects. But more importantly, the rock's rugged bulk is split nearly in two.

It's perfect.

I'm aware that time is ticking by. I run to the boulder and peer into the crack. Within it, I see the darkness I awoke all those years ago. It struggles within the fissure, trying to climb out, but in this window of time still hasn't found the strength to break free.

I jam the pencil-thin cylinder into the crack. I press the release button on the end. The clawed end opens and the spark of time harnessed within descends into the crevice. I see the darkness recoil from the blue light, curling and seething like boiling tar. It looks just like it did on that day so long ago when it broke free of the cracks.

I remember it flooding out, hungry and searching for any sentient consciousness it could claim. And how its evil spread, rising to infect the sky, hiding the sun from us. Across continents, millions died. Their bodies still litter the streets of cities and towns alike. All empty vessels, a macabre sort of discarded clothing, non-decaying bodies awaiting a dark demon's consciousness to claim them for reanimation.

The blue spark floats deeper into the rock, the thin crevice lit by its brilliance. I see the darkness pull back further, but there's nowhere left for it to go. I step back. The crack glows bright blue for an instant and then the spark is quenched.

I hear crickets in the garden. I hear the trickle of water over worn rock.

Then, the granite boulder explodes.

Splinters of rock shower down around me and, along with it, puddles of black goop that writhe and seethe as they hit the grass. The puddles meld together, moving unnaturally fast to coalesce.

Failure.

Again.

And worse, the darkness is now free to hunt me.

"Shit!" I turn and run. My feet fly over the shrubs and onto the gravel path. I hear sloshing behind me. The demons. They are hungry. I skid around the front of the house. I see an old man working in the garden. I almost stop in my tracks. White hair, wrinkled skin and blue eyes. It's John Everton, the real John as he was in the days before he was killed.

"Whoa there, son. Go easy," he says as he notices me rounding the corner of the house. "What's the rush?"

"Run!" I manage to gasp. But he doesn't, his brow only wrinkles in confusion.

"It's all right, Gwenda here will fix whatever is ailing ya'." He reaches down and picks up an old shotgun. I recognize the weapon. It is the one his corpse was holding back in my future. And while his bravery is admirable, the weapon will never hold back the demons.

"Get inside!" I scream as I veer past him, heading for the house.

My tone moves him to action.

Still holding the gun, he turns and sprints, easily catching up to me. He's spry for an old man. We take the verandah steps together, two at a time. The front door is open, the foyer beyond welcoming. In moments, we are inside. I slam the door shut.

"What is it?" John's voice is a whisper.

But I have no chance to answer. The foyer turns dark as the black tar crawls over the glass windowpanes.

"Dear God," John stares at the white, razor-edged teeth within the darkness pressed against the glass. The glass cracks—a short, sharp sound—but the pieces hold in the frame. At least for the moment.

There is scratching at the door. Serrated claws and teeth hidden in the tar gouge at the timber. Soon the dark demons find their way in.

Their tar spreads like ink across the polished timber floor. The stain grows quickly, pulsing its way toward us. John, still holding the gun, starts to pull wicker furniture forward to barricade the doorway leading to the corridor. I grab a polished timber desk and add it to the pile. The tar has almost reached us. I jump up onto the desk. I grip John's wrist and try to help him up but a lick of tar grabs him by the ankle. I pull harder but my grip slips. He falls backwards, landing heavily against a couch. The gun discharges accidently, the spray of hot lead catching the entry door and frame blasting them outwards.

"Help!" John's face contorts with pain. "They're eating me!"

They aren't eating him but I know what he means—savage white teeth are piercing his skin, injecting toxins and drawing out his human consciousness.

I leap off the desk and onto the clear patch of floor by his side. I grasp his hand trying to pull him away but as I do a curl of tar takes firm grip upon my arm.

Then my watch alarm sounds.

Time's up.

"No!" The time portal forms around me. The demons are too close! I feel myself being sucked in. Then the ring of blue fire tears me from this sunlit world and transports me back to my own.

But in transit something feels different. I open my eyes. To my horror, I see licks of darkness threaded through the blue fire of the portal corridor. The demons are in the portal. My panic inspires action.

I spread out my fingers and let the threads catch on my fingertips. A trailing mess of darkness tangles around my hand. I ball it up, ignoring the sharp sting of serrated claws.

I am dropped out onto gravel. I turn, shielding my eyes against the portal's brightness with one hand and holding the dark demons in the other. As it begins to fade, I focus my mind and with it twist the axis of the portal. The time loop shifts and a new doorway is torn through reality and out into limbo. With all my strength, I hurl the ball of demons into the portal. A shriek echoes as I fall backwards. Darkness.

***

I am back in my own time. Patterns of light are playing across my closed eyelids. A fresh breeze pulls at my fringe. I don't remember ever feeling so safe. I don't want to open my eyes. I am tired of all the running, the hiding and the fighting. If I must die, let it be like here, like this.

I hear footsteps crunching over gravel.

"Can I help you there, son?" asks a familiar voice. "You're squashing my pansies, lying there like that."

I open my eyes. To my surprise, I find myself

lying in a flowerbed, looking up through the gently swaying branches of a weeping willow. I turn my head. My gaze meets twinkling blue eyes.

John Everton.

"You all right?" His kind face is filled with sympathy.

I struggle upright. "Sorry," I manage to say, "I, ah..."

The old man smiles. "It's all right. I've had few benders in my time, too. Sometimes you just gotta sleep it off where you fall."

John helps me to my feet. I am still in shock. I don't know whether to laugh or cry. Did I really succeed this time? Have the demons really gone? I look around at the impossibly beautiful day. Yes. I think so.

I let John lead me inside, his offer of bacon and eggs for breakfast is too tempting to refuse. The foyer of the house is bright and warm when we enter. John directs me to bathroom just off the corridor.

I realize it's been a long time since I saw my own face. When I look into the mirror, I barely recognize the middle-aged man with brown eyes that have seen too much of life. Grey hair falls across my forehead and my beard is long. I look like the homeless man I am.

I reach over and turn the basin tap on. Clean, fresh water gurgles out from the chrome spout,

over the cracked porcelain and into the drain.
Cracked porcelain.
I freeze.
I lean down and peer into the crack.
Something black is struggling to get out.

14 | The Darkness Has Teeth

THE HUNTRESS OF BUR

Justin Chasteen

The sunrise glazed the woodland and biting frost swelled to a sharpened glare in his eyes. With each slick crunch of his boots, Gligk wondered if he would ever feel his toes again, unable to wiggle them since the night before. He stumbled west with dim sunlight to guide him. This, he didn't mind, but the man he carried over his shoulders would object the moment he regained consciousness—so he headed south.

Gligk cared little about his destination, so long as he arrived with his life. For ten years, he and his comrades had raided the homes of rich widows. They stole coin, horses, innocence of daughters, and jewelry with little to no resistance. It was a good ten years—a fun ten years with full bellies and empty testicles—but Gligk and company had finally made a critical error.

Gligk turned to check his tracks—two lines in the deep snow that looked more like he'd crawled instead of stomped.

The man slung over Gligk's shoulders grunted and yanked his head up. "Does it still follow us?"

Gligk squinted past lanky, naked oak trees stretched deep into the Marrowbone Forest. The sun was rising rapidly, covering the forest with a golden glint. They'd be more visible now if it still stalked them.

"I don't think so, Rat," Gligk gasped. "Haven't heard a thing in a few hours."

"Christ, my leg's numb. How bad is it?"

Rattle's thigh no longer gushed, but dripped blood along the outside of their trail.

"Do ya have any more water?"

Gligk gently propped Rattle against a thick oak, then reached inside his elbow-patched wool coat. He ripped free a leather bladder and dangled it until Rattle yanked it from his grasp. "I kept it close to my gut to keep it from freezin'."

Rattle emptied the water skin, his Adam's apple dancing with each gulp. "So, what the hell was that thing?"

"I dunno, Rat," Gligk said. "We'd only been in the cabin of that huntress for a few minutes, then everything turned to shit. Somethin' cut off Jimi's head. When it hit the floor his eyes were still wide mouth gapin' like a fish. Yorm charged into the darkness after whatever killed Jimi—I guess he thought he'd make quick work of it—but I'd never heard Yorm scream like that. Not ever, Rat."

"You killed her, right? You killed that old bitch?"

"I did, Rat. Killed 'er before we even entered that cabin. Just liked we planned—she was out back cuttin' wood and I buried my knife in 'er before she could see me comin'. But whatever was in that cabin was waitin' for us."

Rattle grimaced. "We rode in with four horses, and you didn't have time to grab a single one?"

"You were out cold when I found you. I tossed you over my shoulders and ran. I never looked back. Do you remember what happened?"

"No," Rattle gruffed.

Gligk glanced down at the gash, hidden under a crimson-soaked cloth wrapped just above Rattle's knee. He grew weaker with each needled breath that filled his lungs. They'd not last much longer in this chill if Rattle couldn't walk on his own.

"Where's your rifle?"

Gligk ripped at his right shoulder. "It was here before sunrise, I swear. I must've dropped it."

"Christ," Rattle muttered. He winced as he reached into his coat pocket and pulled out a revolver. "I've only got two shots left."

Gligk crouched near his comrade. As long as Rattle lived, they stood a chance against whatever hunted them. "Only need one shot, Rat. You're the best marksman in—"

A thundering blast deafened Gligk, leaving him stunned. Rattle's head, blood and brain, splattered Gligk's face like a monsoon. His ears rang and hands trembled as he clawed gore from his eyes. When he opened them, he saw Rattle's headless corpse squirting blood, shattered skull fragments wedged into the tree like shards of glass.

Only a few paces away, a young girl no older than ten years of age stood before him with a blunderbuss in her left hand. Her expressionless face was pale, bearing a slight cleft in her chin and surrounded by two brown pigtails. The girl spat brown muck out the side of her lips. It wasn't the tobacco that confused Gligk, but her decision to rest the blunderbuss atop her shoulder instead of aiming it at him.

Gligk slowly raised his hands into the air; his fingers tingled from the sharp, blustery morning chill. "Now listen lil' girl. I ain't—"

"You're the one that killed my nana?"

"N-no. I jus' was—"

The girl leaned back on her left leg and pointed the muzzle at Gligk's gut.

"Wait!"

She didn't fire, but the gaping mouth of the blunderbuss remained steady.

"Go on." She spat, brown spittle trickling down her chin.

Gligk knew he had but a moment to plead his case. "We were starved. We knew of your grandma's history."

"So, you killed her instead of asking for a hot meal?"

"We were afraid. The Huntress of Bur was never kind in the stories, lass. We thought she'd kill us for steppin' on 'er property."

The girl spat.

"You're not the first, you know. Not the first to come to our cabin and try and rob us bare."

Gligk's bowels twisted, and his legs grew weak as he fumbled for lies to explain.

"Back to the cabin slowly. You'll dig her grave and bury her."

Gligk glanced at Rattle's headless corpse. Blood still spurted from his neck. "Okay."

Several hours later, Gligk stumbled into the backyard of the huntress' cabin. The girl followed ten paces behind, never lowering her blunderbuss. The body of the huntress wasn't where she'd fallen with the knife in her back, but blood stained the snow near the chopping block.

"What'd you do with the body?" Fear kept Gligk from turning his eyes to the child. There was no way she moved the old woman on her own.

"Look at the track marks, fool. I put her on my sled and pulled her inside so the bears didn't mess with her. Now start diggin' or I'll shoot."

"Where's a shovel?"

"Use your hands," she replied, then spat.

***

The sun squatted in the east, a golden blanket over white branches as far as they eye could see. Gligk had pried enough of the frozen soil from the ground to please the girl. His hands were numb and bloody. If she let him live, he'd lose at least half his fingers to frostbite. A small price to pay considering what had happened to Jimi, Yorm, and now Rattle.

With the blunderbuss steadily aimed at his head, the girl strode to the hole and spat inside. "Deep enough."

Gligk nearly fell to his knees, overcome with relief. The huntress' corpse would be dug up by nightfall in a grave only as deep as the girl's knee. Whatever roamed the desolate forest would surely smell the rot—even from a frozen corpse—but he wasn't about to object and make more work for his dead hands.

He turned toward the cabin and squinted. "You want me to go get 'er?"

The girl took three steps in front of him, spun on her heel, and fired. The blunderbuss unloaded hot lead into Gligk's groin and his feet left the ground. He slammed against the frozen soil and strained, unable to draw breath as he gawked from the bottom of the hole. The little girl spat, and the Huntress of Bur stepped beside her. He couldn't see her face behind the massive hood she wore; grey pigtails protruded from the bottom.

"How's your back, Nana?"

"It'll take more than a knife between the shoulders t' kill your nana."

"Should I cover him up?" Her hollow eyes climbed to meet her nana's.

"No. Bears'll get 'im with the trail of his friends I left from thicket to cabin."

Gligk tried to speak but his mouth was stale; his throat burnt as if he'd swallowed an ember the size of an apple.

They watched on as he struggled to draw breath. His midsection was now numb, but his back ached as if the winter worms were burrowing into his spine. He wanted to murmur a prayer. He wanted someone to save him, not put him out of his misery. But the huntress was his only God now, and she would grant no mercy.

The girl glanced up to her nana and smiled, then returned her gaze to Gligk as she spat into the grave. The huntress, her face wrinkled from a thousand winters, didn't budge or show a lick of pain. Her stare was colder than the soil beneath Gligk, more painful than the lead in his crotch and gut.

His sight started to fade, a shadowed hue circling the two as they were the lone audience to his death. Just as all turned to darkness, the huntress opened her mouth. Pity? A prayer perhaps?

"You hungry?" the huntress inquired. "We got horse stew now."

The girl spat. "I'm starvin'."

FRY MACHETE'S MONSTERS, MUNCHIES, AND MAYHEM

Stuart Conover

"So, when I'm in California, I like to take a load off and have a good time. If I'm at the beach, I want to get something quick and easy. What's easier than a food truck when you're just looking to kick back your feet and soak in the rays? Not much!

"If you've got a taste for something a little different than your standard dogs or may not be quite of the human persuasion . . . I want to introduce you to the 'The Cryptoid Truck' which has been serving the hunger of all types all day and all night. It opened a couple years ago by two of the most unlikely of friends and they have cornered the market on this ghoulishly fun and original take on finger foods.

"With a mobile meat wagon and a tolerant attitude, they've been able to dominate the late night scene. At least for those brave enough among the living, dead, undead, dying, and even some merfolk to keep things fair across the board. You can find a little of everything here in this rolling sliver of SoCal and it's all coming up right now on "Monsters, Munchies, and Mayhem."

The camera cut and Fry Machete sighed as he leaned against his 1996 Lamborghini Diablo and lifted his sunglass to rub his weary eyes. He might feasibly live forever at this rate but thirteen seasons of crossing the country showcasing food joints for the fiendish wore thin, even on him. One would have to make a deal with the devil to find this much success and keep ratings up after so many years. Or, if not the Devil, maybe a deal with the next best Evil God out there available on short notice.

Of course, any deal like that would come at a price as Fry knew all too well. He had a job to do, though, and not sucking up to the audience at the other end of the cameras. No. His real job involved slaying some of the monsters that lay in plain sight among the human populace and fed off them. The information came in packets he had mysteriously been receiving since he had started hosting the show. The ones that linked together murders which had been committed by the nightmares made real. The ones kept secret from the public and, per his latest batch of information, death was sticking to The Cryptoid like white on rice.

Looking at his reflection Fry slowly slid the shades back over his eyes. They were rimmed with almost the same color red as his short spiky hair.

He couldn't sleep from the hunger, again, but the last thing he needed was the studio to think he was on drugs. Again.

The Nom Network might not be able to fire him but they could make his life a living Hell if they so choose to.

While he had been on the wrong side of substance abuse in the past, that was when he was trying to hide from starving all the time. He had no plans to spend another six months getting clean from a drug he was no longer on. These days he was just hungry.

All he wanted was a snack and his stomach rumbled in encouragement, but that was one craving he wasn't willing to satisfy. Not again.

Just as his frustration kicked in, Fry's assistant bounced up. Her overly positive nature and unlimited surplus of energy had him convinced that she wasn't human. At least not purely human. He couldn't ask, though, HR policies and whatnot. The last thing he wanted was a lawsuit on his hands.

Discrimination against nonhumans was a hot ticket for the blood-sucking lawyers these days. Hell, it was even worse than sexual harassment. Whoever had thought it had been a good idea to let vampires have equal rights in the legal system had really ruined it for everyone else.

God, how he hated them all.

Sighing, he threw on a smile as Karen opened

her mouth and still couldn't help but wonder what creature could be so wickedly happy all the time. Better yet, who he had pissed off at the network to be stuck with her.

"So, Boss, I think you're going to really like this one," she said. "I was just talking to the chef and not only do they cook everything in pure lard, but the rumors are its human fat!"

"Humans are animals" he muttered though she steamrolled on. Maybe she hadn't heard, or was just completely ignoring him.

"Of course, they won't say what kind but you can imply the Hell out of it. Inspections being what they are, they couldn't do that without labeling it, but it'd be a great sound bite or two for the show."

Fry did everything in his power to keep the smile plastered on his face for her as his stomach did summersaults. Ratings. It always came down to ratings. That was her job, though. It was just hard to focus on that with the rising need to feed.

"That's great Karen, I'm sure to use that. What were the specials today that I needed to bring up?"

She looked down at her clipboard, blonde bangs covering her eyes and Fry swore she still watched him.

"It looks like some spicy deep fried eel kabobs called The Electric Eel. You'll try a mystery dish known only as The Teasing Tentacle. It is a squid tentacle stuffed with their secret recipe. Finally, you'll have some garlic crusted crustacean on a stick. They call it From Another World for the different flavor that pops in your mouth with each bite. Though, if there's time, they also want you to talk about the Deep-Sea Challenge eating contest that they have."

"Does it look like things have gotten bad enough that we're going to talk about food eating contests?"

A fire burned in his eyes barely concealed by his sunglasses as he pointed a finger at her.

"I'm not that desperate for ratings."

"Sir, I was just thinking—"

"NO!" He cut her off. "It's bad enough that we're still doing this traveling roadshow. I'm not going to cheapen it even more with that inane drivel. There are already other shows on another network for that crap."

"Yes, sir." She bit her lower lip and turned to go. "Oh, and you're expected inside in three minutes."

Shit. He was going to hear about that little outburst from the studio. Any time he outright disagreed with Karen he heard from them. At least he hadn't let out his little digs on another network's show in public. Or, even worse, on film.

Sighing, Fry readjusted his shades, put on a saccharin smile, and walked up to the back door of the truck. He hated filming in these things. Hot and cramped as is, imagine adding extra lighting, a cameraman, and Fry's enlarged gut. No one could truly be happy during shoots in food trucks. Hell, half the kitchens they were in were too small.

Not even thirty seconds passed before his forehead was beaded with sweat.

Just Wonderful. This is shaping up to be an absolutely fantastic night. I can't wait to see how much better it can get.

Fry had just finished filming in Chicago and he hadn't yet adjusted back to the stark contrast in temperature. Things were quite different from the Still-in-Winter-Spring and the 70 degree nights here at home. The Windy City had always had bad winters, but ever since global warming had really kicked in the winters of the Midwest seemed to last forever.

Not only that, but the snow made it that much harder when there was a killer on the loose.

Fry had no idea why the suckers still lived there. What kind of an idiot would put up with the cold when there was still plenty of places who considered fifty degrees a cold winter?

Two men were prepping food for the cameras for filler shots on the show. The chefs had the same uncomfortable posture of everyone who ended up on Triple M and didn't look naturally laid back while cooking. They were trying too hard. Everyone wanted to be Fry.

At least he wasn't going to have to coach these

two that much for the camera.

The chefs were both showing off and Fry finally cleared his throat to get their attention.

They looked up and excitement broke out on one of their faces while the other didn't look as if he knew how to be excited. Clearly, he knew which one spoke to the customers. He wondered which of these two fresh-faced looking pups was in charge.

"Fry!" the younger of the two shouted out. Of course, when so many nonhumans out in public, age became too difficult to guess anymore.

Fry stuck out his hand to shake theirs. He wanted to see if he could tell by touch if they were human or not.

"Johnny Applegate," the first said while vigorously pumping his fist.

The second man slowly wiped off his hand before reaching out with a little too firm of a grip and a smile that didn't quite reach his eyes.

"Dakota", Mr. Personality said simply before looking away.

"Like the state?" Fry prodded and forced himself to not wince as Dakota's grip tightened to where it almost crushed his hand.

This one didn't feel human no matter how well he had the appearance down. Maybe Fry had found the killer he was looking for.

"Yes, just like that" the grip finally loosened and gave one last solid squeeze before letting go. Dakota glanced up for a second before looking away and Fry couldn't read the look.

Fae weren't that strong, and vampires avoided open flames. Perhaps he was a shifter of some type. Fry needed to know exactly what kind of monster Dakota was before he could take him down. Oh, and if it was responsible for the rash of recent customer deaths. Fry couldn't just go out and kill one of them just for not being human no matter how much he might want to.

That would make him no better than they were.

"So, fella's," The smile crept out of Fry's voice. "What exactly do we have going on?"

Applegate immediately jumped in with his gaze bouncing back and forth between Fry and the camera. A far too fake of a smile was plastered on his face and the words were coming out of his mouth at a mile a minute.

"Whoa, whoa, whoa, home slice," Fry held up his hands. "You're going to have to slow your roll just a second there."

So much for not having to coach either of these two to look good on camera.

"The smile and enthusiasm are great but, while one of my friends may always want you to kick it up a notch, you still need to act natural. Act human," he paused and looked at Dakota, "Do you talk to your customers that fast?"

Applegate clearly understood and calmed down

so the two could develop a rhythm. That let Fry's mind wander. He would have to find out what species Dakota was and get him away from the cameras before he made his move.

Fry probably wouldn't get anything done before they finished shooting the episode.

With a few takes on the first dish now on film, it was time to switch things up and get a pre-commercial attention grabber in.

"I've got to tell you those Electric Eels were off the hook. When we come back, I'm going to share some Garlicky Crustacean on a stick with these gentlemen and we'll be finishing things up later with the mysterious Teasing Tentacle." He oozed the last three words out in a suggestive tone and raise of an eyebrow. "It's all coming up when we return to 'Monsters, Munchies, and Mayhem.'"

"Cut!"

"'Scuse me for a second, fellas, It's hotter than Hell in here." Fry walked off. he had started to figure out a plan to get Dakota to out himself.

Clearly, Dakota wouldn't be in the kitchen if there was something in it that could hurt or expose him. Fry had a plan figured out for that, though. A potent dose that mixed silver, sulfur, Siracha, and mayo. Not enough to injure someone but more than enough when taken together to expose most of the nonhumans out there for the monsters they really were.

Making sure no one was paying close attention

to him, Fry slid a capsule out of his car and debated grabbing a weapon, too. The enclosed room in the food truck could work to his advantage, though. Most of the cooking items could double as a weapon in a pinch.

He walked back to the food truck there was a huge smile dripping off Fry's face. His pulse quickened as he knew that he was nearing in on his target. He often felt that in another life he would have been a natural born hunter.

Or serial killer.

He buried that thought.

Fry kept telling himself that the killing wasn't for pleasure.

He had to do it.

Not just as revenge for what had been given to him, for what had been taken in return, but because lives were at stake.

He didn't understand the bargain that had been struck until it was far too late. All he knew is that the monsters had to pay. Especially those that were hurting innocent humans.

Striding into the truck, his pulse was racing as he tried to decide how to get the tablet into something Dakota ate. And a way to get some of the creature's blood.

Though it looked like that last part wasn't going to be a problem.

Fry almost laughed when he saw Dakota

tightly holding his hand while Applegate scrambled to get a first aid kit open.

Fry noticed it was a small cut but deep enough to see that the blood was a dark crimson. Natural. This wasn't the blood of a shifter. Besides, if that's what Dakota was he'd be healing already.

"It's not too serious to pass up being on the show, I hope," Dakota said watching the crew as they finished bandaging Chef's finger.

"Oh, absolutely not!" Applegate cut in, "As quiet as he's being tonight, this is all Dakota has been able to talk about for the past month. Ever since we found out we'd be on the show."

Fry was puzzled. That didn't seem like the man before him, or how a killer, would react. Still, Fry was sure that whoever was committing the murders was related to this food truck. Perhaps it was one of the patrons?

Fry looked out into the sea of faces for those waiting for food and his stomach growled. He tried to tell himself it was from the futility of investigating in the day he had here, and not from the hunger that gnawed at him.

Like it or not, he needed to feed before he lost control.

"Well, if you are all bandaged up we'd better get going." Fry stated, "You've got regulars to feed and we've got a show to film."

Fry considered dosing all the food going out, but he didn't have enough pills with him for that.

Besides, there could be any number of paying customers in attendance that weren't human, and he couldn't risk losing the cover of his show for hunting the dangerous ones.

The chefs were halfway through talking about the various shrimp, lobster, and crab that could end up on the daily special when, finally, Dakota poured himself a glass of water. While Fry felt growing doubts about Dakota being anything other than human, he had a chance to figure it out now.

Fry moved in closer, pretending to get a better view of the crab which was being cooked in his honor. He turned back to give the camera one of his trademark looks showing how sneaky he was being. Doing so he made it look like he accidentally knocked Dakota's glass over.

"Well, that has me caught red-handed," Fry held up a pair of the crab's claws and raised his eyebrows." He bent down and picked up the glass before his mark had a chance. "Let me get that for you, home slice."

It was now or never.

Fry turned away and crushed the capsule into the cup as he started filling it with water.

Smiling he handed Dakota the new glass of water and tried not to flinch as the man's fingers brushed against his. The quiet man was far too nervous around him and it showed while he thanked him profusely for the water. Could he know that his reign of terror was close to coming to an end?

Fry took a step back and prepared for a reaction when Dakota took a big swig. Only none came. Fry's heart dropped. He had been so sure of himself.

Dakota wasn't one of the creatures. Fry had to keep the frustration out of his voice so that the real murderer would not suspect something was off.

"Now what everyone wants to know is a bit more about your signature dish, The Teasing Tentacle."

"Well, this is a specialty of my own creation," Applegate said from behind him. "It's a little something I worked out that no one can get enough of!"

Fry swung around just as a tray full of pre-cut tentacles floating in a liquid was being pulled out from a fridge.

"The secret is in the marinade," the young man continued.

Fry stuck his finger in it and put it to his mouth before Applegate could stop him.

"Hmm... it tastes like soy sauce, basil, and..." he trailed off raising an eyebrow and pulling at his goatee, "I'm actually not sure on the rest."

"Well, that's what makes it a secret recipe," Applegate tried to mimic the sly look that Fry gave the cameras. "And if I told you, I'd have to kill you."

They both laughed though Fry suddenly felt

uneasy. Had he been targeting the wrong chef this entire time?

His thought was abruptly cut off as his unease faded to the background. His stomach truly rumbled and Applegate laughed.

"Don't worry, Fry, this'll be ready soon to fill that appetite of yours."

All Fry could do was smile and nod. The hunger had blossomed to new depths and he was using all his willpower to keep it in check.

"What can I say," Fry said through clenched teeth, "Your food just leaves me wanting more."

"Why don't you try the real thing and quit wasting time on just the sauce?" Applegate asked.

Still playing to the camera, Fry was on autopilot as he took one of the tentacles on a stick being offered to him and heartily took a bite. This kind of food would never take the hunger away but sometimes when he jammed enough down it could alleviate the urges he had.

"Mmm . . . This is," he paused to lick off his fingers and knowing that was a mistake the second his flesh touched his lips, "a totally fresh take on squid."

His stomach grumbled so loudly he worried that the camera would pick it up. He clutched his stomach with one free hand to force himself to not double over.

Whatever was in the marinade was setting off

his need to fill his belly.

He had to get out of here, away from these people, and the cameras before he did something stupid. "Cut!" He got out of the truck before bursting into a sprint, Applegate's laughter trailing behind him.

"Fry! What the Hell?" Karen yelled after him, the bouncy enthusiasm in her voice for once nonexistent.

Out of habit, he ran towards his car. On the way, he realized that he was in no condition to drive and switched direction towards the beach. While being a celebrity allowed for certain eccentric actions, this probably wasn't one of them. Fry could feel the camera phones of everyone who had pulled up to see Fry interviewing their favorite food truck trained on him.

Fry knew that he had to get away, but the beach stretched indefinitely in front of him.

Suddenly the pain became unbearable and he pitched forward. He could hear someone approaching him across the sand.

"Stay back!" He rasped, "You have to..."

The pain came in waves and forced him down. He could smell the scent of the sauce in the air. Applegate must have come for him. If he was going to go down in public for what he was, Fry didn't care who the killer was if he could take the bastard with him.

Snarling, he rose to his feet and pounced on

the man standing over him.

Through a dim haze, part of him recognized that it was Dakota he had pushed to the ground before his teeth sank into the man's flesh. That rational part of his mind could only observe. He mostly shut down while the hunger overtook him.

Fry tried not to watch as he tore into the man. He couldn't close his eyes to the life that he was taking but pulled himself back from it and let the hunger take over. In fact, he became so disconnected that he wasn't aware of the cameras that were filming or the people watching.

All that mattered was the meat. Each and every savory bite of flesh that he tore off. The true price for his pain, the unstoppable hunger that he had allowed to build once again would finally be his undoing. As Dakota's life blood gurgled out with his last breath, Fry licked his lips. His mind was awash with the fear of what was about to happen and the hatred he felt for those who had made him this way.

Shakily, Fry got to his feet and turned around. Before him stood Applegate, the camera crew, and Karen who was on the phone. Probably with the police.

"Yes sir, we've got it all on camera," she bubbled, "No, there shouldn't be any problems getting him to agree."

In his mind, Fry knew that he would be lucky

if he went to prison for this. Non-humans found guilty of murder ended up taking a long walk off a short pier.

Karen hung up and bounced up to him before handing him a towel.

"Clean yourself off while we take care of this. I want you presentable when we talk about your new show."

He took the towel and looked on in confusion as Applegate took an envelope from Karen and one of the cameramen started dragging Dakota's body back to the truck.

"New show?" He wasn't sure what to make of it. "What's going on?"

"First off, get that tone out of your voice. After this little stunt of yours on camera, I just got bumped up from your assistant to your Executive Producer," Karen smiled wickedly. "Next, we're about to announce 'Fry's Foodie Fights'. A new show where for the first half of each episode you go around the country checking out and participating in food contests or eating competitions. In the second half, you will host public events that pit foodies in the area you are in against each other."

Fry glared at her with teeth clenched. The smile that crossed her face was inhuman in the sadistic satisfaction she clearly felt at this turn of events.

"Oh, don't give me that look. This is where the money is and we all know how far you're willing to go to earn another buck and have your face on TV." She paused "We're also going to have to talk about your little side project and hunger issues. The first is going to be stopping as the studio feels that you've been too sloppy with your work while the second. Well, the second is why I now own you."

Fry fell to the beach, the sand working its way into his clothes and he didn't even care. As the spring breeze warmed his skin the waves slowly rolling onto the beach carried away his last hope of ever going back to a normal life. With those hopes, the waves also took any chance for revenge against those who had turned him into one of the monsters he despised.

"The studio might have wanted to lower monster killing to help their shows be accepted," Karen said. "But these days it's all about the bottom line."

ONLY IN DEATH

Zoey Xolton

Amara ran blindly through the dark, the fear of recapture giving speed to her frozen feet. Winter's bitter cold frosted her every fevered breath no sooner than it had passed her lips. She cried out as another contraction ripped through her young body with inhuman strength, stealing her legs from under her. Her knees hit the snow-covered earth and she threw out her hands instinctively. Landing on all fours, she narrowly avoided crushing her swollen belly. Her scream rent the darkness, sending birds shrieking into the star-pricked sky.

Gasping for breath, her tears, sweat and blood mixed in fetid rivulets that etched their way down her form, staining her ivory gown scarlet. She shivered violently as she clutched at the pain in her middle with one shaking hand. Her body begged her to rest, but she could not. She had suffered too much, been tortured and used for far too long, to relinquish her fragile grasp on freedom now.

"*Amara . . .*" Her own name was whispered seductively in her mind. "*You are bound to me. I can feel you in my veins and taste you on my tongue. Your fear is like a heady, dizzying perfume on the breeze.*"

Amara gagged and retched, emptying her stomach of its saccharine contents. Even now, the sickly-sweet scent of the Lady's Tongue Lily was strong. Added to all her meals and beverages, its clear potent nectar dulled the senses and pacified the spirit; leaving her helpless and open to suggestion. Wiping her mouth with her cold, damp sleeve, she felt her legs could no longer support her; so, she crawled.

"*Amara,*" came Lord Vyrixian's call again. He taunted her, his very voice compelled her, threatening to weaken what precious little resolve she had remaining. His beautiful, cruel, smiling face materialized in her mind. Her head spun and the darkling in her belly squirmed. In the distance, she heard the unmistakable howl of The Hunt, the hounds of the Otherworld and their armed fae entourage. She cursed.

When she had felt the first contractions of labor, she'd realized that this would be her only chance at freedom. It was All Hallows Eve, if she didn't make a run for the Gateway with the baby now, she'd be trapped forever. In her hastened and desperate escape, she'd left an obvious trail of blood from her chamber door. They'd picked up her scent with ease and were fast gaining on her.

"*No!*" Her heart leapt into her throat and she screamed internally with frustration and pain. "*I will not go back to that gilded cage! I'd rather die!*" She swore, her mental voice flying through the night, striking Vyrixian's psychic shield with surprising force.

***

From his balcony, the fae king's violet gaze swept over the canopy of the forbidding Mirewood. Beneath the stars, his long braided hair gave the illusion of a twisted river of silver, spilling down his back; while the moonlight revealed his handsome smile to be something far more sinister. He tracked the progress of The Hunt, leisurely swirling warm *Sanguira*, the bloodwine, around in his goblet. From his vantage point, the riders' flaming torches looked like fire flies dancing through the shadows of the ancient forest.

"*You carry my heir and he belongs to me. You belong to me.*" He replied after a time, arrogance resonating through their *Sangfeteire*, their Bloodbond. "*You will be my beautiful snow white queen willingly, Amara, or you will be kept a forgotten mistress. The choice is yours. Don't think I won't pry my offspring from your cold, lifeless womb if it becomes necessary.*" Vyrixian inhaled, his nostrils flaring as he savored the potent, primal terror that flooded back to him. She knew very well what he was capable of.

He felt her muscles convulsing against their own volition as his child squirmed within her, seeking release. This progeny, unlike those that had come before, was powerful, already exceeding his wildest expectations. It amplified Amara's *Mindspeech*, a gift no other human he'd stolen before had ever possessed. She was a rarity, and as such, his heir would be even more so.

The mixing of his ancient fae lineage with the stubborn strength of his gifted mortal prize would birth a creature the likes of which hadn't been seen in the Realms in living memory. Such a creature could walk, unfettered, between their worlds at will. For it, the constraints of the Gateway would be meaningless. In his progeny, he saw a weapon and a power he alone could learn to harness.

***

The fae king's favorite labored on. Everything around her was a blur of white and fierce cold. Though she could no longer feel her fingers or toes, the pain in her womb remained vicious and unrelenting. It assaulted her from within, seemingly clawing at her insides. If she could hold on, just long enough to make it to the Gateway before the Witching Hour, then she would be home again. Amara cursed, crying out as she clambered onto an ice slick log and tumbled over, rolling and sliding down the slippery embankment with uncontrolled speed. For a breathless moment, she soared through the air, then landed, arms outstretched, shattering the thin ice of a seasonal pool. Her head struck a submerged rock with a nauseating wet crack. In the space of a single heartbeat the world faded to black and Amara's mind wandered.

The darkness was peaceful. Here, there were no more baying hounds or the thunder of demon hooves. No more whippings and dangerous, beautiful beds. No more pastries laced with Lady's Tongue. No more unwanted attention and no more cruel, roaming hands. Here, even the dark fae in her belly seemed silent and still. She winced inwardly, realizing she'd never make it home now. The Gateway was still too far, and she was truly spent.

At least, she consoled herself, there would be no more pain. Perhaps she could just sleep forever, cloaked in a blanket of falling snowflakes, crowned in the bloody halo of her own long black hair like a floating angel.

In the blossoming gloom of her mind, as the flame of her soul flickered, she heard a small, seemingly distant voice whisper from within her own failing flesh.

I will find a way home, Mother. For you, I promise.

Amara's body relaxed then, sagging into the icy water that seemed to cradle her so softly. With a small smile on her lips, her burning lungs shuddered, expelling their last breath, and she rejoiced.

She was free.

THESE CLAWS DIG SHALLOW GRAVES

Kevin Holton

I feel her tapping at the window. It's not enough to say I hear her. Each time her finger pricks against the glass, a shockwave courses through my house. The pulse disturbs the air, shakes dust from the cracks in the ceiling, leaves the walls trembling at her touch. Her existence is such an aberration that it seems everything, right down to the molecule, is scrambling to get away. Each little tremor fights to rouse me from my dead slumber, and now that I'm fully awake, I know I cannot sleep again.

She has been trying to enter for six nights now, growing more persistent each time. If I survive this seventh night, I suspect there will be no force, on Earth or otherwise, capable of killing me.

Had it not been for a cold snap, the woman would have gotten in on that first night, but I closed all the windows, locking them for good measure. My wife always said this was a needless compulsion as we lived several miles outside of town. We had no nearby neighbors and weren't near a main road, so no one was going to come by to get in. Sometimes she'd unlock the windows after I'd gone to bed, just to tease me. As much as it irked me, I loved this playfulness. I should've known what was coming once she started leaving the doors locked. Our divorce was painful, though maybe a little expected. If we hadn't, her little game might have gotten both of us killed.

There's no point in calling the police. They cannot aid me, even if they were to listen to me. Living on the outskirts as I do means my small-town cops rarely want to make the drive, and will do anything they can to avoid having to respond. An aged recluse can't have much to worry about, after all. Why waste the effort coming out to see a man who is probably just tired of living with the same lonely shadows?

I am not alone now, though. Her rapping reminds me of this. Reminds me of the fact that this constant interruption, this barrage, is set to end tonight. For the life of me, I can't explain how I know. My heart screams, *This ends tonight*, and the crash that causes my house to shudder confirms it. Still, I don't look at the window, because I don't want our confrontation to be in my bedroom. She will be wherever I turn my gaze, any window at all. I've tested this, standing in the center of any given room and whipping my head around, looking out panes on opposite sides of my house, but there, always there!

Her figure lurked behind the glass, watching, amused, as I tried desperately to find one route to the world outside my house that is not blocked by the enormity of her presence. Even on the second floor, she stands, watching, tapping, as if gravity fears to touch her.

Tonight, I grasp my cane, personalized with a heavy pewter handle, and leave my room. I sigh with finality, making my way to the stairs. The second floor was never well furnished—my father didn't believe in decorations or accoutrements, and sold most of what his parents had left behind—but it seems barren now, with blank walls, and doors opening to rooms so unused even the chairs have gathered dust. Creaks and groans echo as I hobble onto the first floor, turning down the hall to face the living room.

There, at the far end of the hall, lies a window, and I can avoid her no longer. My gaze catches her, with those dreaded talons raised to the pane, each a foot long and blackened by all the forgotten sins lurking in the corners of Hell. Her tapping stops, ceasing the infernal clack, clack, clack of a clock counting down to the end. She stares back at me, and it would've been easy to think she was just feral, if seen from a distance. A wild woman with long nails. Eventually, I would've noticed her violet eyes glow, the ones that now widened against the encroaching mane of raven black hair. The curious, ecstatic grin stretching across her dirty, but almost convincingly human, face tells me we both know something is different tonight.

It is not easy to make me feel fear. I did not feel it when mugged and left wounded, stabbed in the back by a man I didn't see, bleeding out on the streets of New York City, nor when a bear attacked my wife during the third day of our honeymoon and I raced forward, striking it on the jaw to defend her. In those and many other times, I faced terrible odds and cruel people, and walked away unshaken, intact, and proud.

In fact, I have only felt afraid twice in my life.

The first time I was truly afraid was on my eighteenth birthday, when my drunken father flew into an incomparable rage, lunging at me with a broken bottle and threatening to kill me. The second was the week I spent facing the woman at my window.

"What do you want?" I know the futility of my question.

In reply, she raised her palms, sliding them up with a harsh squeak of flesh on glass, pantomiming "*Let me in*".

I didn't bother to turn on the lights. We could see each other just fine. My robe seemed to match the tattered rags she wore, both outfits hanging loose around a wiry frame. Mine, from barely being able to eat or sleep over the past week. Hers, from whatever God forsaken activities she had been doomed to perform before being sent to find me. I'd thought of fleeing my estate during the day, but I had little else to my name, and some force compelled me to sleep when the sun rose, rendering me helpless, useless even, until night—and the woman—returned.

As I walked closer, my cane slipped and I caught myself on a cabinet, upon which sat my father's crystal whiskey decanter. It has been empty since I was eighteen, when I poisoned him, then drained the contents down the sink to avoid leaving evidence. The police caught me anyway—it was hard to get away with such a crime when I lived alone with the victim—but I was not charged. They understood why I did it, as did my wife, when I told her.

I was never secretive about this act. I've confessed it, in full, to the few people I've grown close to, and even in divorce Charlotte doesn't tell others. Perhaps this is simply to avoid seeming like a vengeful ex-wife, telling a story that would seem ridiculous to those who didn't know better, all in an attempt harm her former husband's reputation, but I don't believe so. She handled the information well, comforting me, acknowledging that I had little choice, and certainly wasn't in my rational mind anyway.

Still, I have done all I can to balance my karma, performing charity work when possible, donating large portions of my small income, not to mention my inheritance, and, every single night, asking the universe for forgiveness.

I am not religious, but I believe there are forces out there far greater than humanity. While murder can be justified, I doubt it can be forgiven.

Perhaps this woman is proof of that. A long overdue retribution for my crime.

"What? What do you want? Why do you want me?" My pulse races, my palms break out in a sweat making it difficult to hold onto my cane. I let it go, resting it against the cabinet, head swimming, eyes on the decanter, the woman's *tap, tap, tap* resuming, creating waves in the floorboards. "Why are you doing this?" I yell over the increasingly thunderous clack of her talon.

When she pauses again, I look over. Her eyes, those pale yellow-white orbs with violet irises, are trained on me. Her mouth opens in a smile so big she can't keep her teeth together. I can't help but notice that, despite her dirty skin, unkempt hair, and grime-covered claws, her teeth are a pure, immaculate white. Strong and sharp, I can tell, even at a distance.

Then her whole hand slaps down against the glass, sending a shockwave somewhat stronger than before. "Stop it!"

I don't realize what I've done until the decanter has left my hand. It's halfway across the room when I figure out what she tricked me into doing. The heavy crystal smashes my old window to pieces, sailing harmlessly into the yard.

There was only empty air where she'd been standing.

Blood surges in my veins, body coursing with a sudden adrenaline rush, not sure of what I doomed myself to. Turning back and forth, I try in vain to find her, but see nothing. Not outside, not inside, not in another pane. Nothing. She has simply vanished, leaving no black plume to suggest she had ever truly been there. But I know better.

I've seen too much of the world, and know that demons do not leave their chosen victims. They experience no change of heart. Humans are nothing but rabbits, and all the world's a cage. They might watch us run, scurry, jump, even bite back. Doesn't matter. When they tire of our antics, our little necks get snapped without a second thought. I suppose we make a nice stew.

Now, rage has undone me, let the woman in when I spent so long keeping her out. Everywhere I turn, I see space, see nothing, not even a flick of hair in the shadows the moonlight couldn't quite dare to touch. Yet I can feel her all around me, sense a presence coming closer, smell her monstrosity perfuming through the room. My labored breathing does little to help. Covering my hand with my mouth, I listen close, trying to hear her, but I'll sooner hear the fiends scuttling on the floors of Hell than hear her. If she is moving, she does so with an otherworldly silence no human could hope to match.

I'm still looking for her when I feel knives along my back. They don't press in. They just rest there, almost gently. Knowing better than to move, I hold myself, rigid, waiting for her attack, but it never comes. She steps around my side, trailing her talons along my torso, my skin clenching beneath the thin fabric of my shirt. Once in front of me, finally face to face, the woman smiles again.

With this new perspective, I can see she has an average female's height, making her disproportionate digits far more disturbing. One arm dangles briefly at her side and her fingertips graze her calf, just past her knee. Her eyes aren't merely violet, they are a storm of purple, the deep twilight of encroaching night, alight with the last rays of the defeated sun. When she smiles, her face takes on the joyful quality of a child playing with a new toy, or seeing a puppy for the first time. It is somehow... innocent. Even as her sharp claws reach up to press against my face, I wonder, in equal parts, if I had misjudged her and if she had entranced me. If some dark force compels me to sympathize with a monster.

This has long been criticized as my worst quality. My friends, few relatives, they all say I'm too nice for my own good. I heard this quite often after my divorce, with my cousins chastising me, "She betrayed you. How could you just let her go? How can you forgive her?"

I said only that I was showing her the respect she'd shown me. We both knew what she really meant when she told me she was pregnant, just as we both knew my father had castrated me. I was left unable to perform, let alone conceive. That's why I poisoned his whiskey.

I don't hold her accountable for her actions, just as I don't hold myself accountable for mine.

But all the fury in the world couldn't bring me to call him responsible for this. For the hellacious torment that had rocked my house these past nights. The lack of sleep and assaultive sounds that drove me nearly to the brink of madness. Nor could I say, definitively, that he was at fault for the woman who now raked her talons down my chest. Fear remained, a quaking in my bones that she might gouge out my eyes, or eviscerate me, but she does nothing of the sort.

All those nights, I assumed she was evil, her wild appearance and seismic tapping doing little to reassure me, but now I wonder if I'd been mistaken. Her talons are archeologist's tools, studying me, just wanting to understand, probing me with gentle, cautious movements.

Minutes pass before she reaches up, looking me in the eyes, and presses a cold, sharp finger to my lip, just barely hard enough to draw a faint trace of blood. Turning, she hurries off, clambering out the now open window.

Were there ever a moment in my life where I truly doubted my sanity, it would've been this one, but no. I know better. She is calling me away as a gift, and surely any fate is better than my self-imposed isolation, rotting away in that decrepit house. As I stumble to the frame and knock away the fragments of glass still clinging there, I ask, what was it all for?

All the forgiveness in the world doesn't change the fact that I had been betrayed. Used. Abused. I fling myself into the night, newly invigorated, ready to charge forward to the destiny She leads me forward, this strange woman who now commands my whole attention. My leg even cooperates, allowing me to quickly follow, without pain, even though I left my walking stick behind.

It isn't long before she leads me into a thick tangle of bushes. Before I can burst out onto the other side, a cold hand grabs my arm. Whether she'd simply stopped moving, or appeared behind me, I cannot say. Finger to her lips, she holds me there, the wind hushing me as it blows through the canopy overhead. Beyond the bare branches lies a black sky that sheds darkness on everything we do.

Pointing out, she slowly moves the bushes aside, gesturing to a cabin. We're on the edge of Tiber's Lake. There are a few cottages set up for tourists, sports enthusiasts, and whoever else was desperate enough to get away from civilization that they'd want to stay at the lakeside. The grounds are poorly cared for, the hiking paths overgrown, and the wildlife hostile. But there, a few hundred feet away, blaze lights from a couple looking to rekindle old romance.

No, not just any couple. My ex-wife. Her lover. The man she left me for.

I turn back to my companion. She places one oversized hand on my chest. Raises the other, makes a squeezing, crushing motion. Draws that closed fist tight to her own frame. Smiles in a way that isn't hard for me to understand. All I can do is nod. How can I turn back now, when I am so close to redemption?

She presses my cane into my hand. She didn't have it before. I do not question her.

Creeping out of the underbrush, I approach the cabin, making sure to stay out of sight. They're laughing, talking, kissing, facing away from me. Truly, I don't care about her. I forgave my wife. This was never about her. I look back at the tree line. The woman stands there smiling wider than ever. Her teeth shine in the dark. They're the only light I need.

SLIPPED STITCH

KT Wagner

Daggers of late afternoon sun slice through high windows, swirling fiery highlights into the hair of the naked men. Their fists clench around bamboo sticks as they bend over their knitting. Perched on tiered and tiled benches, row upon row, with sweat dripping from corrugated brows, the men do not look at the ones lying prone before them.

I pat my side arm, reassured it's still there. My job is to deliver the winner. By historical standards, the prize isn't much—an easier death—but most work hard to win.

This spectacle occurs five times a year. It used to be once. Maybe that was better; I can't remember with any certainty.

My regular job title is Prison Guard. On spectacle days, I'm the Designated-Executioner. The temporary reassignment is an honor with extra pay and privileges. Last year, my appointment came down from the Chief Justice, days after the last Designated-Executioner went home and shot herself in the head. At least that was the whispered rumor. In the staff room, we sniggered and rolled our eyes at her weakness.

I try to forget that I know these men. Catfish in particular.

Sympathy is considered encouragement, especially with so many watching. Every day, we are warned. At home, I practice a still expression, mimicking the terracotta masks mounted high on the walls.

Across the chamber, Sammie, a new attendant, moves to wipe condensation and gore from the triple layer of reinforced glass. She clears the view for two elderly women in the front row and the looming mob.

I remember when I was like Sammie. The orgasmic rush of power and righteous retribution.

Sammie's proud and wants to hold up a fist to her friends in the crowd, but it's against the rules. Her flashing eyes reflect in the glass, their glow a fever I know well. A shrug of her shoulder toward the condemned and a slight nod to the crowd. A smirk twitches her lips—definitely against the rules—and she turns from the glass barrier.

As the date for this spectacle approached, for the first time in my life I had trouble sleeping. In the quiet of the night, treasonous thoughts burrowed into my brain. I'm no longer sure all prisoners deserve their fate.

I settle into my stern look, arms folded across

my chest, and glare up and down the rows of men. My heart thumps against my ribcage.

The white tile is a canvas, a landscape painted with human fluids, framing the still life prisoner tableau. Tiny movements only, arm muscles twitch, fingers curl and twist. Sporadically, their work ripples.

On the far side of the chamber is a stack of unused corpses. Leftovers from last month. The staff refer to them as Starter Kits, soon to be used up and replaced with fresher material. Only the so-called winner of this display is spared that final humiliation, their remains fed into the fire intact.

I remind myself this is justice, and they chose to commit the crimes.

Back row, far-right, Catfish blinks against the sweat dripping into his eyes. I blink too. My eyes sting and burn in sympathy. I do not choose to feel this way, but logic doesn't help these days.

Catfish broke a recent law, committed a newer crime. He insulted someone or questioned something. The scant details churn in my mind. He's here, therefore he must deserve his fate. Justice is always right.

I can't shake the notion that if I wipe at my eyes Catfish will feel some relief. It's stupid, and I don't dare do it, because all unnecessary gestures are against the rules.

His Adams apple grinds up and down. Crimson splotches erupt on his fish-white neck, like he swallowed a red-hot briquette. I glimpse his curled tongue before he crushes it between yellowed teeth. I can't help biting down in unison. My mouth floods with blood, scorching and sour.

Catfish flinches, tries and fails to catch his slipped stitch. The steaming rope of his craft tumbles wetly to the tile. Arms strain against chains. Watery blue eyes beseech, then look through me as the auto-inject paralyzes him and he slumps to the floor.

Bile burns the back of my throat.

The other men don't move, but necks redden, eyes narrow—everyone except Torch, two over from Catfish. Torch grins. Torch will prevail, because he enjoys this. Winning for him is inflicting suffering. It's not right.

Torch is a murderer. His gaze is steady on the glass. He watches the crowd, performs for them. His thick fingers caress the guts as he knits them into a mat that spills across his lap, onto the floor, and down two levels. Without breaking his stare, he leans forward, grabs Catfish's hair, and drags him closer. Torch claims him, straightens, and let's go. Catfish's head cracks against the tile.

Sammie waves off the other attendant. She saunters over to Catfish, gutting knife in hand.

My breath catches. Catfish doesn't deserve this.

I look away. I've never looked away before. A

scream builds in my chest. My teeth grind.

I look back. Catfish appears unconscious or dead. With luck, this is the end for him. I breathe again.

Torch's steady hands continue to work. His lips stretch—a wide, dark slash that peels back from filed teeth. Slowly, he licks his lips and winks.

The muffled howl is predictable. White-hot outrage radiates through the glass. Torch basks in it. I want to bash in his skull with bare fists.

I turn my head and look directly at the mob for the first time in months, but the glare from the spotlights washes across the glass barrier transforming it into a mirror.

Body armor, heavy and suffocating, encases me and the attendants. We are giant black beetles in the mirror, individuality blurred by the uniforms. My face is bleached and gaunt, a skull on the side of a desert road.

A small shift and the glare exposes another view—the wall of steel mesh embedded in the glass. I blink and force my focus past the barrier.

The judges occupy the front row. Backs straight, grey hair carefully coifed, black robes flowing to the floor, they bear witness to the enactment of their sentences. I recognize the one to the left. She used to volunteer with my grandmother back when craft was therapy, not punishment.

My grandmother's memory recently began

visiting me at night. I don't want to think about her here.

Above and beyond the judges, the tin ceiling is scorched. The cameras in this execution chamber are gone, only the hangers and frayed wire remain. Open seating and live broadcasts spawned protests, then riots. Now, the audience is screened and the reports scripted.

My gaze drops to the forest of raised fists. The glass mutes the familiar howling chant, "Death is too good for them."

I wonder if it's still the same across the street where the roles are reversed. I've not thought about it for a long time.

There are young girls among the faces in the mob, little faces contorted by hate.

No children. It's one of the rules.

"Sammie, there are kids," I gasp out.

"Rule change. Just posted." She grins.

A cyclone of heat scours my insides.

Though she is several years dead, my grandmother's voice rings loud and unwelcome in my head, "I warned you."

I'd laughed, called her a fool. When they placed her under house arrest, I'd abandoned her for a more enlightened circle. I don't know exactly when or how she passed. A next-of-kin tax bill in my mailbox informed me of her death.

My sidearm slides easily out of its holster. My

hand shakes. I hold the gun out, barrel down. I know he is beyond caring, but I do it for Catfish. I can no longer convince myself he was an exception, a mistake that slipped past the authorities.

The mob roars, an angry Gorgon. Its many heads focused on me.

I turn toward the men and allow sympathy to form the expression on my face. Only Torch appears to notice. He leers.

A hard hand clamps my shoulder. The gun is removed from my grasp.

Sammie's voice is uncertain, "Are you ill?"

The room spins around Torch's face. He deserves this. He deserves more than this.

The dull roar of the crowd again reaches my ears. My grandmother's former friend stands at the glass, one palm pressed against it. Her eyes are not fevered, they are resigned. She looks at me and the shake of her head is almost imperceptible. She knows.

I stumble back a step. Perhaps there is another way.

I focus on Torch and speak to Sammie. "It's okay. I felt dizzy. Didn't want any of that lot to think they could take advantage."

Her grip on my shoulder relaxes. I mouth an apology to the judges. A day or two of rest to recover is all I need. I won't allow myself to slip again. At least, not in public.

66 | Slipped Stitch

SPOTLIGHT

David J. Gibbs

Michael loved going to the farm for Thanksgiving. Everything about it excited him, even the long drive. It didn't matter that the farm was a little rundown since his uncle was no longer able to take care of it. To Michael, it was still magical.

He didn't care that the barn leaned to one side and struggled to hold up a badly sagging roof. It leaned so badly the doors no longer stayed shut. Surrounded by the smell of must and decay, he always imagined the secrets the barn held in its dusty heart.

Outbuildings gathered around the barn in a broken sort of worship. The silos stood next to old farm equipment left to rot on tires that had burst long ago and were splayed like blackened rubber flower petals catching the sun.

All of those were special, in their own way, but they weren't the main reason Michael loved visiting the farm. He adored what happened when the sun went down and the shadows swallowed it whole.

The farm changed into a macabre playground. During the day, the barn was full of forgotten farm implements, tools, ladder and dusty rope, but when the sun went down, the open barn doors became the yawning mouth of some slumbering beast. Tree branches with skeletal fingers raked across the metal roof making sounds that slipped beneath his fingernails and poked his soul.

Michael and his cousins played in that playground every year. They were at the back of the house waiting for him so they could begin their game. The late chill nipped at his fingertips making him zip up his jacket.

"Are we doing this or what?" asked Becca, her unruly red curls held hostage by thick barrettes at the back of her head.

"I'm ready," Michael said.

"Who has the flashlights?" Christopher shoved Becca in the arm which made her lose her balance and stumble.

"Nice, little brother," Becca kicked him in the shins.

Christopher slapped the back of Becca's head when she wasn't looking and she whirled on him, offering a quick punch to his stomach.

"Uncle Lloyd said he had a couple," Michael said.

"Don't use his," Becca said. "They suck. He never puts new batteries in them. We should go ask Gary. Maybe he'll let us use his police ones."

Michael said, "That'd be pretty cool."

"I can go ask."

"Is Fred playing?" Michael asked, tossing a stick over a nearby fence.

Christopher laughed. "Why do you always call her Fred?"

"Mostly 'cause it bugs her," Michael said, smiling before adding, "Besides, I don't think she knows my name. Why should I use hers?"

Michael was worried if they didn't get started, the game might end before they had a chance to get it going. He knew his parents wouldn't want to stay long. Neither one of them liked the long drive back in the dark.

"I'll go ask her and see about the flashlights," Christopher said.

"Are you coming back?" Becca asked.

"Yeah."

"That's what you said last year, too," Michael said and they all laughed.

"It was really, really cold last year," he protested, shrugging his shoulders. "And I didn't want to mess up my shoes. It was muddy."

"It's not right the way you collect so many shoes," Becca said.

When Christopher was inside, Michael turned to Becca and asked, "Do you think he's going to stay inside?"

"I don't think so. I think he's bored out here

most of the time. The only time he says he's not is when we play Spotlight."

"It does get kind of boring inside watching stupid football all day."

Becca laughed and asked, "What's wrong with football?"

"Nothing at all. I just can't stand to watch four hundred straight hours of it."

The back door opened and Christopher came down the steps with Fred in tow.

"Gary let us borrow his cop flashlights! Look at these things," Christopher said, blinding both Michael and Becca who held up their hands to shield their eyes. "You're under arrest!"

"You ass," Becca said.

"Language," Fred hissed.

"Ashley, knock it off," Christopher said, and then corrected himself. "I mean Fred."

"Why do you guys do that?" Fred asked, crossing her arms.

"Because we know it gets to you, dork," Becca said. "So, are we playing or what?"

"Duh," Christopher said.

"Duh," mocked Becca back at her brother.

"Who's going to be it first?" Michael asked, already knowing what the answer was going to be.

"You asked, so I say you should be first," Christopher said tossing the flashlights his way.

"Great," muttered Michael, picking up the

flashlights off the ground.

He counted, making his voice loud and dramatic, and looked up at the stars overhead. The moon hung in the night sky looking as if a giant's fingernail had pierced delicate fabric. When he got to twenty, he yelled, "Here I come!"

He looked around him, the night coating everything with a thick helping of shadows. Michael had always liked creepy things. Using the flashlight, he carved a path through the darkness, the outbuildings coming into view and then the barn and the fields beyond. He listened for any sign of movement, any hint that would lend itself to finding the others. Something about wandering around the farm with a flashlight in hand with the darkness hugging him made his heart beat a little faster. His cold hands gripped the metal flashlight, so he pulled his sleeves down to cover them as he looked for the others.

Just as he turned back toward the farmhouse, he heard something scraping against the back of the largest outbuilding nearby. It was the one that had Uncle Lloyd's camper and two other cars hidden in it. Ducking down, Michael turned off the flashlight and moved as quietly as he could. He figured it had to be Fred. She wasn't very good at finding hiding places since she didn't team up with Becca anymore. Michael wanted to sneak up and scare her.

The dry grass crinkled under his feet. He

heard the scraping again and closed in. Her back was to him, her light-colored coat easy to see in the dark. She was hunched down, looking around the corner of the building. As he closed in, he frowned. It was too small to be Fred.

Michael flipped on the flashlight, a splash of light bringing out the red of the barn in the darkness. He inhaled a quick breath, ready to yell, when a solid block of ice filled his chest. What whirled around, mouth agape, in a twisted mask of feathery white, wasn't Fred. It stood about a foot tall with fissures spread outward from the yawning hole that was its mouth. Eyes caught the light with a glittering blue as it raised an arm to ward off the stark white stain of the flashlight. It wheezed and snorted before a fluttering sound burst from its mouth. It lunged toward him with a swipe of its hand.

Michael screamed.

He didn't care that he sounded like his little sister. He dropped the flashlight and raced along the side of the building heading for the wash of light coming from the back porch.

"Help! Help me!"

The thing slithered along in the brush. He could hear its ragged breath and the dry husks of grass crunching under its feet. Michael kept waiting for it to take a swipe at his legs, to make him tumble.

Stumbling into the backyard, he almost felt like he was going to pass out.

Becca slowly came around the row of parked cars. She crouched, as if she thought he wanted to trick them into revealing their hiding places.

"Is it over?"

"What do you mean?" He hunched over, out of breath.

"Are you calling it off?" Becca rubbed her hands on the front of her jeans.

"There's something over there. Something chased me."

"What are you talking about? Are you serious?"

"Yes, I'm serious."

"You sure it just wasn't one of the farm cats?"

"It was not a stupid cat," Michael said, shivering.

"Or Fred?"

"It wasn't Fred and it wasn't Christopher. I don't know what it was. I've never seen anything like it before."

They heard a scream coming from behind one of the silos. Looking at each other, they ran.

"Maybe we should go get Gary," Michael said, his breath coming fast.

"For what? Would you calm down? I'm sure it's just the two of them messing around. There's nothing there. What's wrong with you?"

He didn't answer, instead pumping his legs even faster and pulling ahead of Becca. The chilled night air forced tears from his eyes, but he didn't stop. The pair rounded the nearest silo and almost ran into Christopher and Fred.

"What the heck is wrong with you guys?"

He just looked at Christopher. "What do you mean?"

"You guys running around in the dark, and where is Gary's flashlight?"

"Dad's gonna be real pissed if you lost his flashlight."

"Shut up, Fred."

"Not cool," Christopher said.

"Why did you scream?" Michael asked Fred.

"Genius over here scared me," Fred nodded toward Christopher.

"I didn't mean to. I heard something by the outbuilding and thought it was you, so I was moving to a new hiding spot."

"You were over there by the building?" Becca asked Christopher.

"At first I was, why?"

"That's got to be what you heard, Michael. Christopher moving around over there in the weeds."

Michael shook his head.

"What?" Becca asked.

"That's not what I saw. It wasn't Christopher."

"Then what did you see?" Christopher asked.

He was in dangerous territory. What if they

didn't believe him or, worse, thought he was losing his mind? "Probably just spooked myself."

"Oh, come on. Spooked by what?" Fred asked.

He looked at Christopher who shrugged his shoulders.

"Are you kidding me?" Becca asked.

"I'm going inside to get a quick drink," Michael said, heading toward the steps leading to the back porch.

"What about my dad's flashlight?"

"It's over there." He motioned toward the outbuilding as he went inside. He needed to get out of the dark. His legs were still shaky.

Opening the back door, the warmth from the house hugged him in greeting.

Michael grabbed a cup of punch and, sipping it, he squeezed through the cramped dining room having to slide between the china cabinet and the back of Uncle Butch's chair. Women surrounded the table trading recipes and talking about who was in the hospital and who had gotten married. Talk like that always made Michael want to go outside.

The family room had far too many people in it, but it was the only room in the house with a television. The football game blared to the room full of men and Julie, the only woman boycotting the dining room chatter. As he stood staring at the game, not really paying attention, Michael wandered behind the couch wedged in the middle of the room. He looked into the tiny bedroom off the back of the family room and noticed Aunt Lottie sitting in a chair, looking out through the back window.

"Michael." She didn't turn around.

"Yes?"

"Come in here for just a minute, would you? Sit next to an old lady and tell her something good."

Sipping his punch, he looked around at the people staring at the television. They didn't even acknowledge he was in the room. It seemed like they only reacted to the television. Michael went in to talk with Aunt Lottie. She was always a hoot.

"Why aren't you out playing your flashlight game?"

"Spotlight?"

She nodded.

"I just needed a drink."

Aunt Lottie smiled at him. Was she toying with him?

"Were you watching us?"

He forgot about the punch in his hand and noticed the pane of glass looking out behind the farm house. He shivered. "Aunt Lottie? What's wrong?"

"Nothing, dear. Not a thing. I just wanted to talk to you for a bit. I saw you drop the flashlight." He didn't say anything. "I think I know why you stopped your game."

He swallowed hard.

"There's something that most people don't realize about Thanksgiving. I know everybody thinks it's giving thanks for the Indians who took care of the first settlers. They brought all of these gifts of food. It helped get the people through that terrible winter. But that was just part of it, a very small part. They had something more in mind. It's something that came over from the old world."

What was she talking about?

"Those gifts weren't for the settlers. The gifts belonged to what they brought with them."

"Aunt Lottie, what are you talking about?"

"You know I grew up in northern Romania, right?"

"Of course."

"My village was quite small. Just a few hundred of us wedged in the mountains. It was a hard life by anyone's standards, but I didn't know any better. I worked at a local bakery and thought myself happy. I liked the work, though I found myself constantly dumbfounded by how often I miscounted the loaves of bread."

Michael put the empty cup on the small dresser.

"He explained that these things, these little creatures, lived in the mountains and came down from time to time for a tithing, so they wouldn't feed on the children. They were small, spindly things, he told me, and they mostly ran around on all fours, almost like ferrets. They could stand upright, if need be, to pluck pies from window sills and bread from baskets. Mr. Steinkov said all of this with an odd smile, so I didn't know if I should believe him, or if he shined me on.

"Years later, when we were living here, I found out. We baked the pies and breadstuffs from the old country and placed them to cool on the window sills. Time to time, some would go missing."

"Offerings?"

"Yes. I realized that no matter what my father thought, we couldn't escape the old ways. He told me, centuries before, some of his family left Romania to set up a bakery just outside of London. They had the same problems where things would go missing. They didn't question it, they simply made extra. Well, when the Pilgrims embarked on their journey, the bakery donated goods. They wanted to do their part, of course.

"Unknowingly, the settlers had brought the creatures on that first boat and they were hungry after the long trip. Inside of a month the children started to disappear. In the beginning, people blamed the disappearances on a bear spotted outside of town, but I think even then they had to know. After the fourth child went missing, on All Hallows Eve, they knew the bear had not done it.

"The settlers had also come to realize that something was different about the soil of this new world. The breads did not rise well and the pies weren't as sweet. More of the villagers got sick, and the crops did not take to the new earth as hoped. Shortage of food for the settlers meant the critters didn't get enough either.

"The creatures branched out. Thinning the herd, I think they called it. The Indians talked of strange creatures roaming the night snatching children. They hissed and spit as they dragged the children off into the night.

"In their villages, the Indians made sacrifices and danced to make amends for any possible slights, but it wasn't enough. They wondered if it had something to do with the new settlers.

"The village leaders realized that they needed help to keep the critters at bay. After talking with the Indians, the tribe brought gifts of food, understanding the necessary sacrifices to keep the strange creatures satisfied. The little creatures made sure to leave nothing but crumbs. They were appeased for the time being.

"This day was called Thanksgiving. They were giving thanks the creatures were held at bay."

"I don't get it," Michael said.

"You don't get what?"

"You're saying this still happens?"

She nodded. "Think about how much food is on the table in the dining room right now. There isn't much left, is there? While someone isn't watching, the last few things will be snatched. There won't be many leftovers. There never is."

"How come I've never heard of this part of Thanksgiving before?"

"You weren't old enough to understand it. Not until this year. These things have been around for centuries."

He thought about what she said. Did they all know?

"Do me a favor, would you? I hid one of the pecan pies behind the basket in the dessert room. Put it on the porch when you go back out."

"Aunt Lottie, I'm not going back out."

"Yes, you are."

He looked at her.

"They're still hungry. We mustn't have brought enough food this time. The younger generations don't relish baking and cooking the way we used to."

He'd heard his mom saying the same thing on the way up to the farm this year. The younger women didn't bring the same amount of food the way the generation before had. It felt strange hearing the same words coming out of his aunt's mouth. Michael knew Aunt Lottie acted a bit crazy, everybody in the family thought so, but he didn't think she had made any of this up. Her eyes were clear, her voice steady. He didn't smell liquor on her breath like he had at some family gatherings.

"I need you to put the pie out on the front porch."

They looked at each other and he wondered if she held something back. He liked her a lot. Aunt Lottie didn't treat him like a kid.

"Okay," he said, surprising himself.

"It needs to be done soon."

Michael nodded and headed into the other room. Squeezing behind Butch again, he grabbed one of the pies.

"Good idea." He turned around to see his mom walking toward him.

"What?"

"Take a pie home with us. We're packing up to head out."

"Oh, this isn't for us."

"Who is it for?"

He couldn't tell his mom the truth. There was no way she was going to buy it. She looked at him like he had gone crazy as she waited for his answer.

"I'm just kidding, Mom."

She smiled and ran fingers through is hair. "Better say goodbye to your cousins."

He nodded.

Everyone was so busy talking and laughing that they didn't pay attention as he made his way to the front porch. Once outside, the chill caught him off guard. He hadn't realized it was so cold.

Kneeling down, he pulled the foil off the top with a loud crinkling sound.

"About time," Fred said.

"We were just about ready to come in," Becca said.

"You suck," Christopher said. "I can't believe you made us wait out here that whole time. What the heck were you doing?"

Ignoring them, Michael set the pie up on the railing of the porch and tucked the foil underneath.

"What are you doing?" Fred asked.

"Just something Aunt Lottie needed me to do."

"Steal a pie?" Becca asked, laughing.

"Not stealing it. She just needed me to set this out."

"Why?" Becca asked, coming closer.

"Who puts a pie out on the porch?" Christopher asked.

"Wouldn't birds come and get it or raccoons or something?" Fred asked.

Michael avoided Becca's eyes.

"Just tell us what's going on. Why did you put this out here?"

"Aunt Lottie told me about the things that the Pilgrims brought with them."

Fred burst out laughing.

"What?" he asked.

"You have to be kidding me. You actually bought that crap?"

He frowned.

"Yeah, we all know the stupid story," Christopher said.

"Really?" He was confused.

All three nodded.

"Why didn't you tell me? So, you knew the things were out here on the farm?" Michael asked.

"Wait, wait, wait. No, there's no creatures. They aren't real, you idiot." Becca stared at him.

"But, I saw it. I saw one of those things on the other side of the out building. That's what freaked me out."

"Oh, come on," Christopher said. "It was one of the cats."

"It wasn't a cat," Michael said.

They looked at him.

"It wasn't a cat. And, it wasn't Fred either." He looked at Becca.

"Excuse me," she said, holding up her hands.

"Look, just come on. She said to leave it on the porch. My parents are getting ready to leave, so let's go hide for another quick round of Spotlight."

Fred had the flashlight and handed it to him. He frowned and looked at her.

"You never finished your turn."

He nodded and started to count. When he was done, he yelled, "Watch out. Here I come!"

Michael heard sounds in the barn and made his way without the flashlight to the open doors. He listened quietly and heard whispering. If he had to guess, he would say it was Fred and Becca. He turned on the flashlight and bathed the inside with white light. The truck cap was tilted to one side and then it shifted, letting him see Fred's foot.

"Spotlight on Fred!"

"Aw, man."

Fred came out as he lowered the flashlight and ran into the darkness toward the back of the farm. He knew some good hiding places near the fence line. One of the trees had a nice crook in the lower branches that he could hide in. Just as he rounded the tree, he heard his parents calling his name. He climbed up the tree and wedged himself between the branches.

"Michael, let's go!" It was his dad calling. He didn't sound happy.

Great.

He climbed down from the tree and headed back in. Becca, Fred, and Christopher were coming in from their hiding places, too. Michael sighed. He wasn't ready for it to be over. Shoulders slumped, head down, he dragged his feet back to the house.

A few minutes later, Michael waved to his cousins as his parents drove away from the farm. He usually liked the drive home because he could look up at the stars, but tonight it was a little too cloudy. The darkness swallowed up all the light.

As he settled in for the long ride, using the pillow he brought to prop up his head, when he heard something behind the back seat.

"Stop it, Michael," his sister spat, slapping him because his leg brushed hers. "This is my side, that's your side."

"Shut up!" he yelled suddenly.

"Both of you knock it off!" His dad glared at them in the rearview mirror.

"You need to settle down," his mother added. "You're lucky we didn't spank your behind right there in front of everyone."

He heard the sound again and sat up listening carefully.

"Are you listening to your father?"

"Yes."

"Why didn't you put the pie in the van like I asked?"

He heard the sound again and knew what it was this time. It was crinkling foil.

"You just left it out on the porch. The foil came off and everything. It would've been ruined. You were just off in your own world playing Spotlight."

Michael wasn't listening. Instead, his mind was filled with the sound of foil crinkling just behind his seat. It was easy to picture the small hands working their way beneath the foil to the pie, stuffing handful after handful into its twisted mouth.

"Are you listening?"

"Michael? Mommy's talking to you!" his sister yelled.

"Quiet."

"If I wouldn't have picked it up we wouldn't have any pie to eat."

"Mom, no."

"Don't tell your mother no!" his dad yelled, his voice filling the van.

"You don't know what you did. No, no, no."

He heard more crinkling and then other sounds he didn't know what they were, until his sister squealed, "Something's pulling my hair! Make it stop!"

"Michael, leave your sister alone!"

"Mom, it's not me."

"Make it stop!"

"Scoot over toward me a little bit. Your hair is probably caught in the seatbelt."

His parents were still fuming, but at least they were doing it in silence. He could still listen for anything moving behind their seat.

"Thank you, Michael," his mother said quietly.

He realized she just thought he was being nice to his sister not trying to keep the thing behind them from eating her. It was maddening hearing that crinkling sound over the course of the four-hour trip with his imagination running wild. Every time Michael thought the thing had finished the pie and had started looking for something else to eat, the sound would come to his ears again and he'd relax just a bit.

They pulled into their driveway sometime around midnight. As he fumbled with his seatbelt and his mom unbuckled his sister who had fallen asleep, Michael heard his dad pop the back hatch.

"What the hell?"

"Language," his mom said, waking up his sister as she unbuckled the seatbelt.

"Sorry. I just...you need to come here."

Michael tumbled out of his seat and ran around the back, his mom and sister joining them a moment later. His dad pointed to the pie— or what was left of the pie. The aluminum foil had dozens of holes through it and the edges of the pie pan were crumpled and crimped. Michael looked at the pan, his dad tugging the foil away from it. There was nothing left. It had been licked clean.

"What happened to the pie?" His mom asked.

"I don't understand. We covered it up before we left. I know it was a full pie," his dad said, squeezing the back of his neck.

One of the garbage cans fell over in the side yard with a big crash.

"Stupid raccoons," his dad said, leaving them to stare at the empty pie pan while he stormed off into the darkness while the foil moved in the breeze.

Michael's eyes widened. *That was no raccoon.*

COYOTEMAN

Robert Perret

I was killed on the evening of August 23rd, 1981 by two transient tweakers by the names of Randy Mitchell and Lurlene Simons.

That was a first. I'd made a little hobby of cruising the I-12 back and forth across the state line, through the Bitterroots. Find me some latter-day hippies, drifters or hobos, hitchin'. Seeing that outstretched thumb, the international sign of the parasite, it always put me in a hunting mood. I'd drive them out on some back road. A shortcut I'd tell them, or a scenic route if they didn't seem to be in a hurry to get anywhere. I'd kick them out of the car, give them a 20-minute head start.

The trunk of my reliable old Plymouth Duster could hold four adult bodies in a pinch, so my own corpse was spread out in relative luxury on its lonesome. It was some sort of purgatory, I supposed, to be here in my own trunk listening to these two dipshits having their little Bonnie and Clyde adventure. They'd knocked over a drugstore in Lolo. Some geriatric pharmacist handing everything over at the first sight of a pistol, no doubt, but to hear them tell it, these two were real banditos.

And I did. I had no choice, tethered to a dead body like I was. I'd first seen Lurlene off the side of the road. Long brown leg propped up on the guard rail, jean shorts cut off to Hallelujah, flannel shirt knotted up between her tits so her bellybutton seemed lost in a sea of taut skin. She arched her back when she stuck her thumb out, fanning herself with a straw cowboy hat in the other. She was a living pin-up meant to get some trucker or farmhand all hot and bothered. Me, I just saw a hundred greasy, hairy schlubs grabbing her, grinding up against her in my mind. It sickened me.

When I pulled over she leaned into the passenger window, all sweat and perfume and cleavage, while Randy came creeping up out of the ditch beside the road. It was a standard ploy, gas, grass, or ass as the bumper sticker says. Guess which gets picked up the quickest. I pretend to be chagrined and they pretend to be apologetic and away we go.

They are talking way too fast and laughing way too loud. I'm kicking myself. Tweakers are terrible game. They either lash out right away, putting all the fun to an end as soon as it starts, or they sit gibbering in the first hole they can find. It's all short-term decision making and no strategy, like hunting a squirrel. I didn't drive two hundred miles into the middle of nowhere to shoot a squirrel in its hidey hole. What am I supposed to do with them now? Fuck it. I'll drop them off at the Denny's in Missoula and pray for better hunting on the way back. Besides, he's passed out in the back and she's rubbing up against me and cooing. Her whorestink makes my dick shrivel, but it's an academic exercise in how far she'll go. It is intellectually satisfying to know I could, even if on a physical level, she repulses me to my core. She seems like she is sobering up, working the junk out of her system with her trailer park ingénue routine.

I start to think maybe this is good for target practice at least. I casually suggest, "Hey, let's get off the highway and go up Miller Creek. There's an old fur trapper trading post out there, these fucking Mr. Wizard medicine men , they got a whole lab up there. Bring this shit in from Canada, refine it, purify it, enhance it. They are like wholesalers, cut out the middleman."

True to form, she is game. Too eager, in retrospect.

I've never been to this crack shack but I've heard about it enough times. It's like Mecca for the ticks I pick off the road. She falls asleep with her head in my lap and I turn the wheel eastward. In an hour, we are there. They must smell the drugs in the air because Lurlene and Randy both perk up about the same time.

We can see the lights of the post flickering through the trees. They must spend a fortune on gasoline to keep the place lit by generators. The place has the whole log-cabin-surrounded-by-a-wall-of-pointed-logs thing going. There's even a U.S. flag on the flagpole, through it is upside down and defaced with an anarchy "A". I feel a twitch in my eye. Good men died for that flag.

As we drive through the gate we are eyed by thugs embracing machine guns on either side of us. Everyone inside the compound is armed, too, whether with a rifle strung across their back or pistols at their hips or both. I tell Randy and Lurlene to get out first. These whackos will get spooked by a straight-laced square like me. I grin to myself, seeing a gunsight on every head in view.

I breathe deep and slow. I'm a predator in the night, not a SWAT team. Sure enough, my freaky tweakers exit without incident, but hands grab guns when I get out of the car. I hold my hands up and give a friendly double wave while slowly spinning in a circle to show I am not armed.

One of the guards points his chin at the door of the fort and we go in. The room is lit by a hundred Bunsen burners. It is a fantastical world of beakers and flasks and gauges and scales, somewhere between Merlin's workshop and a moon base. At the center on piles of rugs on the ground sits a circle of Indian elders. They gesture for us to join them. A peace pipe is passed. The smoke is acrid and chemical. Randy takes a deep puff, Lurlene takes two. I pantomime drawing from the pipe.

As my eyes adjust to the darkness I see skulls ringing the room. Bison and moose, elk and deer, all in a mosaic. As my pupils expand to take the dim light in smaller skulls become visible now. Human skulls, with snake skulls shoved in the eye sockets. We are surrounded by a thousand silent screams. Randy and Lurlene are too high to be scared. They bray like idiots and the Indians stare passively at them. I meet their savage stoicism unshaken and stone cold sober and we recognize each other as predators.

The circle appears to be headed by some sort of medicine woman. She tosses crap into the fire that sparks and smokes and calls upon the ancestors to bring good fortune and smile upon this transaction. Randy and Lurlene get the giggles. The old woman produces a knife, giant and serrated. The handle is huge. It takes my mind a moment to recognize it as a femur with animals carved into it. Crows and coyotes and jackrabbits, and feathers tied by a leather thong to the end. She says their ancestors were done wrong by the white man and that their avenging spirits rest in this knife. The trade will be fair or vengeance will be had.

Randy and Lurlene are still giggling like idiots.

The medicine woman suggests negotiations be opened. Randy surprises everyone by opening his duffel bag and dumping stacks of cash on the ground.

"We'll take it all," he said, and he and Lurlene begin cackling uncontrollably.

One of the guards appears and stacks the cash up into neat piles, counting as he goes. He announces a figure in some savage tongue. The medicine woman nods. Behind them tapestries depicting buffalo hunts or some such thing are moved aside and a bank style vault is revealed. With a sharp clacking and ponderous turning a great wheel is spun back and forth. The vault swings open and Randy and Lurlene gasp.

There are bricks of powder and baggies of crystals and envelopes of who knows what sitting wall to wall, floor to ceiling. Many of the onlookers seem impressed. The vault must not get opened so publicly very often. The medicine woman has just begun to offer quantities when Randy shifts and locks an arm around her throat. The other arm holds a pistol to her head. Lurlene is giggling and pointing her gun to and fro. Bonnie and Clyde here had Saturday night specials shoved down their trousers. Dime store guns for dime store hoods. The guards have their big boy semiautomatics trained on us. I slowly put my hands out and lay on the ground, trying to look as unthreatening as possible.

Randy reiterates that he wants it all. The guards posture but it is clear they will not fire while he is latched onto the old medicine woman. He yells for Lurlene to grab the cash and for me to start loading up the car with drugs. I take two armfuls and start doing the math. This will take hours. The shock is going to wear off. These people are going to scalp us and eat us alive. I decide to capitalize on Randy's mistake of sending me to the car first by peeling out of there and leaving them behind.

I feel a dozen barrels pointed at me as I plod forward. At the trunk, I awkwardly juggle everything around to get the keys out of my pockets, like a frazzled mom at a grocery store. With my two armloads dumped in I try to casually sidle around to the driver's door. Just then Randy and Lurlene come bursting out of the post, dragging the medicine woman along as they back towards the car. Many of the people who had been inside swarm out into the night. They have guns in their hands and murder in their eyes. The shock has worn off. They are ready and willing to kill us.

"Get in" Randy yells at me.

I do, revving the motor. Lurlene hops in the passenger side, throws the duffel of cash in the back seat, and starts bouncing up and down making little claps. Randy falls backwards through the open rear window like a scuba diver, pounding the back of my seat and practically speaking in tongues. I see the glint of the ancestral knife in his hand.

"You are crazy," I howl. "Jacking their drugs is business. Stupid business but still. Taking that knife, that is an act of war. You have signed our death warrant."

"They don't know who we are," he replies.

"This is my car."

"You are fucked then," he says and they laugh.

I put the pedal to the floor and we whip through the night at twice the posted speed. The chassis scrapes the ground, the sides are torn to hell by trees and rocks. At least one of the struts is shot by the high-speed jarring. I don't care. As soon as we are within walking distance of Missoula this car is going over a ravine with the bodies of my hitchhikers inside. These dumb fucks robbing an international drug cartel like it'sthe corner gas station, all smash and grab.

I feel the knife at my neck.

"Pull over," Randy says, his fetid breath hot on my ear.

"Are you crazy?" I shake him off like a horsefly.

"Off the road, lights off, we'll be fine."

"I'm sorry he doesn't know how to ask nicely," Lurlene straddles my right leg and runs her hand down the front of my pants. "But I know how to ask very nicely."

"Knock it off", Randy smacks her with the back

of his hand before bringing the knife back up against my neck.

"You had those waitresses in Casper, let me have some fun too," she pouts.

"We're hiding this shit and then we can all go into town and have some fun, okay baby?"

"I don't want that kind of fun," I say.

"Shut up!" they both yell at me.

We pull up the next logging access road, just ruts really where a truck-width space had been cleared out.

"I saw you have a shovel in the back," Randy smacks me in the back of the head with the pistol, "start digging and no funny ideas."

I pop the trunk and sure enough, beneath the drugs there is my faithful shovel peeking out from beneath the blanket that covered my kill kit. I was just inches away from knives, gun, chloroform. Maybe it wasn't too late to have a little fun with Lurlene after all. Then Randy's gun was pressed against my head again.

"You're thinking and I'm telling you thinking is real bad for your health right now," he said.

I gingerly got the shovel out. These two have trouble keeping their focus for long. I'd get my chance on the backside when they were bored and too antsy to pay attention. Randy dictated a spot a hundred feet into the trees and I dug while he carved lover's initials into the tree and around that a pentagram. That seemed like asking for trouble to me but hey.

As I figured, Randy got bored and grabbed the shovel away from me, yelling that I was going too slow. He attacked the ground with great fury but barely made a scratch in it. Lurlene laughed and Randy turned a dark red. He dumped the duffel bag and the drugs into the shallow grave we had managed and then had me cover it back up. All the while his Crackerjack gun bobbed and weaved in my general direction. He then kicked me and told me to quick march back to the car.

Lurlene traipsed along in front of us. She must have gotten into the goods because she had gone from manic to spacey and then gently caressing the trees and singing to herself as we returned to the car. When we got back she leaned across the vehicle like a beauty queen at a car show. There, in the moonlight, draped across my Duster, she found a certain kind of beauty. I stopped to admire her for a second and that was when I felt the knife slice my throat.

It didn't feel like much of anything. Like that first moment of numbness after slicing a finger on a freshly sharpened blade. I remember the knife snagged on something in the middle, like the vocal cord or something, and Randy gave it a sharp tug. That tug is what I remember. I felt hot blood run down my chest and arms. I felt Randy heave me up over his shoulder and dump me in the trunk. I heard Lurlene ask why they didn't just leave me here. I heard Randy say something about cadaver dogs and bears and keeping the stash safe. He said they'd get a mile or two from Missoula and roll the car off a bridge with my body inside.

For a second I wondered if Randy could read my mind. I listened to their crazy love making as the trunk bounced up and down. The car would need a thorough detailing inside and out. Then we were on the road again. The Duster pulled heavily to the left. The suspension squealed and the tires burned. I had no doubt we were leaving miles of telltale tire tracks.

We stopped, muffled whispers came from outside. They moved towards the trunk and I heard Randy put his foot down that it would be worth it to move my body to the driver's seat. I shook my head in disgust, and that simple motion made me aware of my body again. The trunk popped open. The moon framed Randy's silhouette. The pale light tingled on my skin. My fingers twitched, my eyes flickered, a smile twisted my lips. Randy noticed and cocked his head. When I made no further movement, he shrugged and heaved me up over his shoulder. I felt the studs on the shoulder of his jacket dig into my stomach. I gave my head a couple of small experimental turns.

The moonlight was like a healing fire on my back. I felt my strength coming back. My fists clenched. From meat I had been made man again, and then more. I could see everything, every grain on Randy's soiled leather jacket, every crag in the bark of every tree. And I could smell, the metallic earth beneath us, the rank water below, the animal scent of Lurlene, it was all so vivid to me now. Randy flopped me into the driver's seat. The knife was there in the middle, still bloody where it had cut me.

He reached across me. "Can't forget my little souvenir," he said.

Seeing this white trash waster touching the sacred blade triggered an ancient lust for vengeance. I pinned him to the roof with one hand, the smell of his fear exciting me, and expertly scalped him with the knife I found in my other hand. The blood dripped down on me and it was glorious. Randy was screaming, Lurlene was screaming, Lurlene was running. I shoved the knife into Randy's heart and twisted the blade. He fell silent. I tossed him aside and hopped up on the car.

In the moonlight I saw Lurlene scamper into the darkness. Yes, there was my prey, the hunt I had been longing for. I had killed the deceitful white man and would take his woman and kill her, too. The farther she ran the sweeter the kill. I saw the lights of Missoula on the horizon. Those artificial lights, scars on my hunting ground. I was hungry for vengeance against these trespassers,

these hitchhikers, the parasites.
And I would have my fill.

THE KILLERS

Meredith Schindehette

I thought it was the end. I felt a piano wire wrapping itself around my head, creeping inward and outward at the same time. Slowly. Intentionally. I'd never felt anything like it.

I closed my eyes and let the darkness wash over me. The pressure crushed me with its intensity. Just short of unbearable. Nothing stopped, though. In fact, everything vibrated. My heart pounded. My mind raced. My body hummed. But the end I thought was so near, wasn't even close.

***

I woke up curled in a ball on the floor of some old-school Toyota pickup. The all-weather car mat indented my left thigh and a few strands of hair stuck to the glove box. I blinked and tried to figure out what happened.

The truck smelled of damp vinegar and looked about as clean as a truck that old could be. I shifted my weight to alleviate the pins and needles attacking my left foot, and to get a better view of my situation. I brushed some hair from my eyes and unwittingly ran my fingers through a sticky mat of bloody fringe glued to my forehead. I willed myself not to gag.

I took a deep breath and looked around from my vantage point on the floor. A tan cloth interior with the passenger seat covered in plastic, automatic transmission, and manually controlled windows, —not a speck of dirt on the floor mats, nor dust on the air vents— convinced me that whoever owned this beauty was practical, unassuming and maybe just a little anal.

All of a sudden, I heard a garage door shut and my natural light was replaced by fluorescent bulbs shining through the windows. I heard voices and strained to listen to their conversation.

"You shouldn't have brought her here. We're supposed to meet at the barn. You know that."

"I know, but she's awake, and the barn is too far away."

The voices were low, but they sounded urgent. Troubled.

"Help me get her out. She can't walk."

I heard scuffling then the tailgate jolted open, rattling the truck. Quiet whimpering floated into the air as someone climbed into the covered truck bed.

"Gently now."

"Cover her with this." More scuffling.

"Okay, now . . . One, two, three."

The whimpering turned into a full-fledged whine that nearly broke my heart.

"Over here. Here. Okay, shhh. You're alright. Just rest now. It's okay." Then more quietly, "Thank you."

I heard clinking glass and small, squeaky wheels, a refrigerator opening, and a freezer hissing. It sounded like a whole lot of commotion for a couple of people and some sort of animal. After a while, though, the racket died down and the whining stopped.

I stayed hidden in the cab the whole time, desperately trying to think of a way out of this mess. I heard footsteps along my side of the truck. My back stiffened, and every kinked bone in my body screamed for attention.

"Um...there's something else."

"What do you mean, 'there's something else'?"

"Well, uh, I mean there's someone else. Um, in the truck."

My mind raced. Hiding in here until they left and then sneaking away just vanished as an option.

"Jamie, this is out of control. One at a time. That's what we agreed."

"I know. I just...this is different. She's different. I found her in the ditch, but she's not totally broken."

"Not broken? Then she shouldn't have been in the ditch. Actually, why were *you* at the ditch in the first place?"

"That doesn't matter. I don't know why she was there. That's why I brought her back. I think we can help her, and then, well, maybe she can help us."

"Jamie. No one is here to help us. I told you before: we're on our own."

"That's not true! Just look. Tom, just look."

The handle cracked and the door creaked open. *Somebody should oil that.* I shut my eyes as the artificial light flooded the cab.

"Oh, my god."

"No. I know what you're thinking, but she's okay. We can fix her. She's not completely broken. I know she's not. Come on. Please."

"Jamie, only broken people go to the ditch."

"I know, but . . ."

"She's broken, Jamie. You need to take her back."

No. He needs to let me go.

"You're wrong."

And that was that.

I felt a gentle tug at my shoulders and then a pull from under my arms. Jamie was trying to get me out of the truck. I kept my eyes, and my mouth, shut. *No use in stirring the pot just yet.*

He laid me out on the floor of the garage. It radiated a smooth coldness, like someone had sealed it with epoxy. He wiped my forehead with a rag. His hands felt warm and gentle despite their rough texture.

"I covered the seat with plastic, so she wouldn't get any blood on it."

"Yeah, I see that." Tom grumbled, but at least he wasn't forcing the issue of dumping me back into whatever ditch Jamie found me. "Jamie, you have to stop going to the ditch. It's not safe. Someone might see you." He paused. "Then what would happen to us?"

"I'm sorry. I know. I'll try."

Jamie hovered over me, his breath puffing in my face. He smelled like vinegar and sweat. I didn't care much for that combination, but I imagined Tom would smell sour and moldy. Jamie became the lesser of two evils.

I lay quietly letting Jamie rearrange my limbs and pick the dry blood out of my hair. He was meticulous. I imagined myself as Humpty Dumpty, his eyes darting over my pieces as his hands worked to put me back together. I relaxed a bit, just enough to realize that I didn't feel any pain. Not since the piano wire. Given how deep the cut felt at the time, I thought I would hurt a lot more.

"Do we have any tape?" Jamie's voice sounded mechanical.

"Huh?"

"Tape. Like surgical tape and gauze?"

"Yeah. I think so. Hold on a second." Tom rustled around the garage again, grunting every so often and mumbling to himself. I thought about the poor animal from the truck bed and hoped she was okay. At least I knew Jamie and Tom helped those in need. Like me.

"Here."

"Great. Thanks."

I knew I would have to open my eyes soon. I couldn't keep the charade going much longer. I just wished I knew what had happened to me.

After Jamie fixed the gauze to my inexplicable head injury, I knew I had to give up the game. I blinked. The fluorescent lights hummed, and their energy seemed to flow into me. The garage was too bright. I couldn't see too well. Everything seemed fuzzy around the edges. Jamie helped me sit up.

"Hi, Mama," he said, and he kissed my cheek.

Tom spun around so fast he knocked a bunch of cleaning supplies off the workbench. He gasped and turned white.

I looked at each of them. Jamie was just a boy, a teenager, maybe sixteen. Tom was older, in his forties, I think. I could see they were related but not sure how. Brothers. Cousins, perhaps. Father and son? I couldn't tell.

Tom didn't look at all like I expected. He was

quite handsome even with the dumbfounded look on his face.

"Jamie. How?" he stuttered.

Jamie couldn't stop smiling; he seemed almost giddy. His wide hazel eyes looked so familiar.

"Told you she wasn't broken."

I tried to stand, but I felt so wobbly. Jamie held my arm. His long, lean muscles tightened like a runner's as he helped me. Despite his strength, he held himself too humbly. His innocent expression and eyes that blinked too much reminded me of someone naïve and easily manipulated.

"Mom, here. Sit down." Jamie guided me to a metal folding chair near the workbench.

I forced a smile and tried to speak, but no words came. My throat was scratchy, and my mouth dry. I still felt woozy, but my eyes had adjusted to the light so I could see better. Tom stayed silent. He seemed so adamant earlier that Jamie should take me back to that ditch. I figured now he would march us back to the truck and send us on our way. But he didn't. He just looked at us like freaks.

Again, I tried to say something, anything, but I couldn't. Only a sort of guttural moan, nearly a growl, emerged. Tom's eyes widened, which seemed impossible because they already bulged farther out of his sockets than I thought possible.

"Jamie, this isn't right," Tom lectured. "Your

mom is gone. No one is here to help us. We live on our own now. This." He gestured to me. "This is not Mama."

"But it *is*, Tom. Look at her. Just *look*."

Tom took Jamie aside and whispered. I could see his chiseled jaw straining as he chastised him.

"I know you think it's her. But Mama's gone. She's never coming back. When you find someone in the ditch. They're broken. They're always broken."

I wanted to stand and defend Jamie. *I'm not broken*. But it took all my strength not to fall over as I sat on the chair. Jamie turned and looked at me with his sweet face. Tears welled in my eyes. I wanted to hold him, tell him I loved him. My heart leapt. *I love him*. My first memory returned. He was my son. I still didn't remember Tom.

"Even if it's not Mom," Jamie paused and swallowed hard. "She can still help, right?"

Tom looked at me and grimaced. Then he turned his head and looked toward the back of the truck. I followed his gaze across the covered bed of the shiny beige pickup to the front wall of the garage.

There, across a dark blue vinyl-upholstered medical examination table, laid not an animal, but a woman. She looked unconscious and the IV in her arm was attached to a saline bag. She appeared to be in her late twenties or early thirties and had a cast on her leg. Her long, perfectly brushed hair looked angelic fanned out across her bare shoulders. She wore an off-the-shoulder top with white cropped jeans and no shoes.

Tom cleared his throat, and I refocused my attention to the men. I could feel another memory surfacing, but it hovered just out of reach.

"I don't think she wants to help us, Jamie." Tom sounded condescending again. "She didn't want to help us before, remember?"

"But if she's different now, if she's not really Mama . . . Well, maybe when she was broken, she changed, and then I fixed her, so she does want to help."

Good reasoning, Jamie.

I smiled. Tom frowned. Jamie moved to hold my hand.

"Okay, look. You don't have to decide right now. She's not strong enough anyway. I'll take her somewhere no one will find her, and when she's strong enough to help, then you can see if it will work. Okay?"

Tom didn't seem convinced, but he couldn't argue with Jamie, not if he wanted more of his help later. Even though he was the epitome of tall, dark, and handsome, Tom apparently needed Jamie's brawn.

"Fine." Then he turned and walked towards the girl on the table.

Jamie bent down to my ear and breathed, "Yay!"

I squeezed his hand, and a smile spread across his face to light up his eyes.

***

The truck jolted forward and soon we left the garage riding a dirt path down a slow incline. Fields of dry weeds peppered with sunflowers and poppies lined both sides. The sun shone and warmed my cheeks. The clouds dotted the sky, billowy and white. I longed to open my window and take a deep breath. But Jamie warned me to keep the windows shut, so no one could see me through the tinted glass.

At least Tom let us go. He told Jamie to take me to the far side of the river near an old barn and lots of trees. He said it should protect us from prying eyes. So off we went, me to figure out what happened and Jamie to help me get back on my feet. Literally.

As we crept along the path, my legs stuck to the plastic-covered passenger seat. I opened the glove box hoping to find a cloth or napkin I could use to wipe up the sweat but as soon as I had it open Jamie reached over and shut it.

"Tom doesn't like people to see the stuff in there," he apologized.

I got the sense that Tom had many things to hide. In the mere second it was open, the glove box surprised me especially since the rest of the truck appeared spotless. Papers, pens, wrappers, bags, scissors, a knife, binoculars, and dirt spewed out the instant it opened. I didn't find anything useful to unstick my legs, though.

We had a bumpy ride, and Jamie kept apologizing.

"Ugh. Sorry. You okay? I don't want to hurt you. Are you sure you're okay? How do you feel?"

I still couldn't talk properly, so Jamie just listened intently to my series of grunts like he could understand. He peppered me with questions for a while and then quieted. He looked lost in thought.

"Mom?" He said it so softly I almost didn't hear him over the noise of the engine. "I want to show you the ditch."

I looked at him and nodded, my head flopping forward feeling very unattached to my neck.

"I just. I just think you should see it."

I grunted, and he accepted that as my agreement to his proposal. A thousand questions ran through my mind as I shifted in my seat.

"Just don't tell Tom, okay?" He didn't take his eyes off the road.

Of course, I won't.

"'Cause it's kind of just outside of town, and Tom would be really mad if someone saw us there."

Right.

"We'll keep the windows rolled up, and we won't stop for long. Just so you can see it."

Okay.

"When I was little and you were, um, you. I would get scared every time we passed the ditch. But you would always tell me to be brave." He bit his lip as he reminisced. "You would say that everyone goes to the ditch someday. It's nothing to be afraid of."

I hope I was right.

"You were right," he blurted as if he knew my thoughts. "You were in the ditch, and now you're here. I don't care what Tom says. Not really."

We pulled onto a curb and drove through iron gates into some sort of garden. Old oak trees guarded the entrance, and moss dripped off stone buildings as we drove past. I couldn't see a sign anywhere, but my body ached the instant I saw the chiseled grey monuments. They dotted the hillside in front of us, rows of permanent sentinels.

I could see why they called it the ditch. The lines of tombstones ran down the grassy hill and up the other side of the shallow valley. Ditch was perhaps a harsher word than I would use for this tranquil meadow, but I understood. After the initial wave of fear, I felt at peace. Sort of. Except for the slow crawl of searing pain creeping around my head again.

Jamie broke the silence. "I found you there." He pointed to a dirt patch in a plot marked by a single-family headstone. He drove slowly, winding his way along the path until he came to the marker. I held my breath. Then I saw it, —freshly churned earth piled into a rectangular section of the family plot. A grave.

I was buried alive?

Jamie parked the truck in the narrow lane. My heartbeat drowned out the rumble of the idle engine. He turned to me.

"Tom said you didn't want to help us." He searched for the right words. "I know you and Tom love each other. I mean, he's your brother, so of course you love him because that's what family does. But...when he brought you here, I knew something was wrong." His eyes watered, and he whispered. "Just wrong."

My brother buried me here?

Jamie scanned the valley ahead and then shifted into gear, but I needed more answers. I jerked forward and put my hand on his arm. He looked at me with tears in his eyes and then bowed his head.

"When you said you didn't know what Tom and I did every weekend, I told you. I brought broken girls to the barn. Tom fixed them and sent them home. I thought you knew. You left to talk to him, and you never came back."

Jamie sobbed. "He told me you had broken.

But he couldn't fix you. I found you in the ditch. He put you there. He just covered you with dirt. I dug you up and brought you home. I don't think he thought I could fix you. But here you are. Not perfect, but here."

My heart seized, and the whole world seemed to stop. Tom tried to kill me. I discovered what he was doing, —all those missing girls, and he tried to kill me for it.

Jamie and I looked at each other. His face held remorse; mine, anger. We both jumped when we heard another car rumble down the path, the dirt and pebbles churning under the rubber.

"It's Tom!"

He saw us; we couldn't hide.

"Our windows are up. We're just visiting the ditch. He can't be mad at us for that."

I knew better. I reached for the handle to open the door, but Jamie stopped me.

"No, please. Let me talk to him."

I didn't know how I would confront Tom in my mangled state, so I had to let Jamie go.

Okay. You can handle it.

Tom got out of his car and slammed the door. I could just see a flash of blonde hair behind his seat before his door closed. Jamie jumped down from the truck to meet him, and as he spoke he seemed more confident. I heard him say that he brought me to the ditch to see if I remembered anything, but I didn't.

"She doesn't know, Tom. She doesn't remember, and I didn't tell her. She asked if we were going to help the girl in the garage, and I said, 'yes.' That's it. I swear."

"Jamie, you know she wanted to stop us from helping those girls, the ones who need us. Even if she doesn't remember now, she will someday. And then what? What are we going to tell her? That we got into an argument, and she ended up in a grave? She'll never forgive us. She'll never forgive you. You told her that we took the girls. You made her worry. You broke her. We have to do what's right. You know that. That's why you brought her back to the ditch. I'm very proud of you for bringing her here."

"Um. Thanks. I…I thought you'd be mad."

"Mad? No. I'm not mad. It was the right thing to do, and now I can finish what you started."

"What I started?"

"Yes. And when that's done, we can go back to work." He looked back at his car as if he were checking to see if something —or someone —was still inside. "You can pick them up, and I can fix them. They get to go home better than before."

Then, as if he were testing Jamie, he asked, "You didn't let her out?"

"No. We kept the windows rolled up. No one saw us."

"Good."

By now, I had drenched my plastic seat with sweat, and I felt my body slip towards the floor. My breaths came fast and shallow. My heart raced while my head spun in tight circles.

Tom tried the handle on my door. Luckily, I had locked it when I leaned over to get a better view of the ditch.

"Come unlock this for me," he commanded, but Jamie didn't budge. "Jamie?"

Jamie stalled. "What are you going to do?"

"I told you. I'm going to finish what you started."

"But I didn't start anything."

I pulled up on the lock as they spoke across the hood of the truck.

"You brought her back."

I opened the glove box.

"Here, to the ditch."

I grabbed the knife.

"You know she's not the same."

I unlatched the handle and creaked open the door.

"She needs to stay dead this time!"

I careened out of the truck and smashed the door into Tom. He lost his breath and staggered back. I jabbed the knife up and punctured the side of his head. His face reverberated with the blow. He blinked in disbelief. I attacked in high speed while the rest of the world stumbled after me in slow motion. Tom had no time to react. Whatever shackles held me back from owning my limbs before vanished. He could not protect himself from my brutality.

When I stopped, Tom laid on the grave in perfect form. It looked as though he could be swallowed by the earth, into the pit from which I came.

I turned to see Jamie's face frozen in twisted shock. He stared at Tom's lifeless body then raised his eyes to mine. I dropped the knife and stumbled toward him.

The side mirror on the truck had broken off; it probably happened when I rammed the door into Tom. I bent over to grab it and caught a glimpse of my reflection. The reflection of a killer. As I studied myself, I didn't recognize who or what I saw. Blood spattered my cheeks. A dark red wine scar cut across the top of my forehead. My eyes seemed bloodshot, my lips were swollen, and bruises mottled my face. I looked dead.

I heard Tom's voice in my head. "She needs to stay dead this time."

Stay dead?

I remembered my voice, the growl, a groan, a moan. I wasn't buried alive or left alone in the ditch.

I was dead.

Jamie brought me back, so I could help him.

And I did. I killed Tom to free my son.

    I fell to the ground, to the pile of earth and bone. I looked up at him, my Jamie, my love. The darkness came again. This time it consumed me.

ANNABEL LEE

Erin J. Kahn

For those of you who do not believe in the permanence of the heart's affections, I offer the following as evidence. Know that it is of the truest nature, and do not suspect, because of the story's strange and unnatural elements, that I have constructed a fiction. If you doubt the veracity of my tale, I ask you to reflect on whether I could, of my own volition, have made up a story of such a peculiar nature. If I could have invented a series of events so unlike anything I have ever encountered. No, this story is true, and for proof I lay it before you; its utter strangeness will vindicate me, if my initial argument does not.

It was on a dark and gloomy evening in late October—indeed I believe it was the 31st—when I forever bade goodbye to the beautiful Annabel Lee, the sweet companion of my innermost heart. For years, I had courted her, wooing both in springtime and in the bleak dregs of winter, until she had, at last, consented to be mine. A short measure of happiness was ours, filled, however, with such a concentrated stream of golden bliss that I knew many lovers both happy and unhappy would have envied us. When my dear wife conceived, I scarce could breathe for joy, but the son and heir of my estate did not enter upon the threshold of my world before bidding it goodbye forever, and my sweet companion followed him before two minutes had elapsed. Was it forbidden for a man to know such a high and unearthly happiness? It may well have been, for in the intense delirium of love, I surely worshipped Annabel above God.

    These were the thoughts that occupied me as I stood alone before the grave of Annabel Lee. The gloaming gathered to a murky darkness in the air, and the vaporous mists of day hung low to the ground. Meanwhile, the night's shadows lurked behind every tree and tombstone waiting for their hour to come.

    In the spirit of the holiday a few straggling revelers, unwilling to return to their well-lighted homes out of the chill evening, kept up a macabre chanting and cheering that reached me faintly on the wind: a demonic incantation punctuated at times by shrieks and howls of an unseemly nature that would have disturbed me had my thoughts not been so entirely occupied elsewhere.

    Eventually, as the shadows lengthened and stretched upon the night, a silence grew so profound it caused me to raise my head. The revelers had retired to their warm hearths, and I was left entirely alone in the cold forest of the night. I knew, to my heart's quailing, that no warm light burned for me.

Nevertheless, I knew that I should return to my solitary house. Bidding a last goodbye to her whom I loved, I turned my back on the grave and began to walk home through the gloom. The air was chill and dank with mist, and I had the sensation of being in a nether sphere, neither here nor there, but in somewhat of a ghostly existence between the world of the living and that of the dead.

In this netherworld of mists and vapors, I became gradually aware of a sound like the slow plodding of feet on the road behind me. Some reveler, I assured myself, lost in the dark, or seeking to scare any who traveled the road at this deep hour of the night. I drifted on through the mist, and the footsteps continued in the intervals of my own.

The footsteps were light, just barely touching down to the road, as if the traveler stood tip-toe or walked with a very light tread—tap-tap, tap-tap, tap-tap—a slight person with thin shoes, or perhaps none at all. As I listened, I deduced the person on the road behind me was most probably female, and indeed, her bearing was not unlike that of my late Annabel.

For some reason unknown to myself, a sudden

dread of my follower filled me, and I broke into a sprint in order to lose her. I ran down the road for a good fifteen minutes before halting beside a phantasmal willow tree, my breath escaping in short bursts, visible on the chilled night air.

    I stifled my breath and listened to a heavy silence.

    Tap-tap, tap-tap, tap-tap, came the footsteps on the road behind me. No farther off in relation to me than they had been fifteen minutes before.

    I resolved to face the unknown person and, summoning all my resolve, I called out: "Who is it trailing me? And what is your purpose?"

    I received no reply. The footsteps had halted.

    "If you mean to scare me," I continued. "Your efforts are wasted. Go find a more timid subject for your experiment."

    Again, no reply.

    I waited for the tap-tap, tap-tap on the road, but only silence greeted me. A chill ran through my blood.

    Suddenly a tremor passed through the spectral figure of the willow tree beside which I had halted. It began at the tips of the long hanging tendrils, touching them faintly as if with a ghostly wind, but the leaves began to quake more forcefully, sending a dry rustling into the air, until the willow was shaking in a violent fit of rage. The strands of willow brushed against each other with a noise like that of the rocking of the sea in the grip of a storm, and I pressed my hands into my ears to shut out the deafening roar.

Then, almost as suddenly as it had begun, the willow ceased shaking.

Slowly I lowered my hands from my ears and felt the overpowering stillness of the night like a heavy muffler around my brain. A cold stream of air glided past me, brushing my cheek with an icy hand.

"Annabel!" I cried in utter despair. "My love, is it you?"

The grass beside the road rustled fitfully, the briars at my feet twisted their scrawny twigs against each other, the willow trembled. A thin moan grew out of the night, rising in volume until it was an audible cry, a shriek, and then a hoarse and husky wail, like the exhalation of a corpse carrying on the nether wind to my ears.

I felt my total incapacity to move, as if a grip cold as iron had seized my limbs. A red film spread over my eyes, and my bones chilled and hollowed within me. A dullness coated my blood, and in increasing desperation I struggled to fill my lungs with air. I felt the touch of invisible yet unmistakable fingers, small and unbearably cold, on my lips, followed by a short rush of breath that smelled of the stale inside of a coffin and entered my lungs with a dizzying coldness. Against the deadening weight around my brain I struggled to direct my thoughts to the God I had forsaken.

    A cloud shifted and the harvest moon appeared in the dark folds of the sky, throwing a thin beam of white light upon me. A sharpness came into my mind, and the weight eased from my limbs. In my newfound strength, I bolted from the phantasmal force that held me and ran with all my might down the dark road. A horrible cry followed me on the air, and an urgent tap-tap-tap-tap echoed against my ears, but still I ran without casting a look behind. My lungs burned, my breath heaved like jagged iron against the inside of my chest, and still I ran. In the shifting shades of the night I beheld the figure of my own house, leering like a grim visage out of the fog. The tap-tap rose to a thunder, sounding nearer and nearer as my breath quailed, and an icy touch clipped my ear. I reached the gate, fled up the front steps, and threw wide the door, hurling myself in and thrusting the door back behind me. It clanged into place with a metallic thud. All settled into stillness.

    I fell to my knees under a wave of weariness, casting my eyes over the silent and empty interior of my house, the ashes cold and dark on the hearth. Looking about me, I found no remnant—not a trace—of the beautiful Annabel Lee.

ABOUT THE AUTHORS

Justin Chasteen

Justin Chasteen was born and raised in Ohio. At the age of 31, he started writing fiction, and now at 33 has a Bachelor's Degree in Creative Writing. Aside from "The Huntress of Bur," he has both an Honorable and a Silver Honorable mention from the L. Ron Hubbard Writers of the Future Contest, a flash fiction story titled "The Shattered Galaxy" (River & South Review), a best-selling short story titled "The Old Man Next Door" (Write Out Publishing), and four completed manuscripts of various novels (which he now regrettably needs to edit for future publication).

Justin also covers high-school baseball and football for the Daily Advocate newspaper. Justin enjoys being a music snob, reading fantasy, NFL football, training boxing, and going on quests through the wilderness with his four-year-old son, Owen—a retired toddler model.

Stuart Conover

Stuart Conover is a father, husband, rescue dog owner, horror author, blogger, journalist, horror enthusiast, comic book geek, science fiction junkie, and IT professional. With all of that to cram in on a daily basis, it is highly debatable that he ever is able to sleep and rumors have him attached to an IV drip of caffeine to get through most days.

A resident of the suburbs of Chicago (and once upon a time of the city) most of Stuart's fiction takes place in the Midwest, if not the Windy City itself. From downtown, to the suburbs, to the cornfields—the area is ripe for urban horror of all facets.

David J. Gibbs

David J. Gibbs is a Cincinnati native whose work has appeared in dozens of publications, including Sanitarium Magazine, After the Happily Ever After, The Sirens Call, Under the Bed, New Realm, Massacre Magazine, Dark Monsters, Tales From

The Grave, Hidden in Plain Sight, and Shadows of Salem. Later this year, his work will appear in: Broken Bones, Those Who Walk, The Monsters Within, and Depraved Desires, among others.

His piece "Mr. Garret's Interview" won 2015 Story of the Year from FictionMagazines.com.

Links to all published works, free stories, blog, news, and updates are available at his website: www.davidjgibbs.com.

Kevin Holton

Kevin Holton has published more than 100 short stories, poems, and critical works. His writing has appeared alongside the likes of Lisa Morton and Ray Bradbury, with companies such as Siren's Call Publications, Crystal Lake Publishing, and Thunderdome Press.

When not writing, he acts, teaches, and is finishing a Master's degree. His free time is spent cooking and talking about comics.

Pamela Jeffs

Pamela Jeffs is a prize-winning speculative fiction author living in Queensland, Australia with her husband and two daughters. She has had her short fiction published in various magazines and anthologies including the *The Outback* by Boolarong Press, *The Lost Door* and *Nocturnal Natures* by Zimbell House Publishing, and the forthcoming *Lawless Lands: Tales from the Weird Frontier* by Falstaff Books. Pamela is very proud to now also have a new work included in the Mighty Quill Books's anthology *Dead of Winter*.

When she isn't being a writer, Pamela has a background in Interior and Exhibition Design where she has had the good fortune to work with a multitude of talented artists. This exposure has given her an appreciation for art in all its forms, including graphic and sculptural, as well as the literary.

For further details about Pamela, visit her at www.pamelajeffs.wixsite.com/pamela-jeffs or drop her a line via Twitter @Pamela_Jeffs.

Erin J. Kahn

Erin J. Kahn lives in New York City, where she works as a copywriter for a news and entertainment site. Her short horror story "Haunted" is forthcoming in Fantasia Divinity. She also co-authors a literary and arts reviews blog at woodbtwntheworlds.blogspot.com.

Robert Perret

Robert Perret is a writer and librarian living on the Palouse in north Idaho. He prefers classic horror and retro slasher stories, and thinks the Pacific Northwest has more to offer than vampires and Twin Peaks, although both of those things have their moments. He reads and writes primarily pulp genre stories and Sherlock Holmes pastiches. His fiction has been featured in Two-Fisted Librarians, Spicy Library Stories, An Improbable Truth: The Paranormal Adventures of Sherlock Holmes, Curious Incidents: More Improbable Adventures, The Science of Deduction and in many other collections. More information can be found at robertperret.com.

Meredith Schindehette

Meredith Schindehette has a BA in English from UC Berkeley and a MSc in Media and Communications from the London School of Economics. After more than two decades working for companies around the world, she now escapes her responsibilities to author horror and speculative fiction stories while locked in her basement. After her kids go to bed, she regularly eats cake and watches horror movies with her husband in their Colorado home. Occasionally, you can find her tweeting @meredithwho.

KT Wagner

KT Wagner loves reading and writing speculative fiction. Occasionally she ventures out of her writer's cave to spend an hour or two blinking against the daylight, or reacquainting herself with family and friends. Several of her short stories are published, and she is working on a sci-fi horror novel.

She puts pen to paper in Maple Ridge, B.C., organizes Golden Ears Writers, and attended

SFU's Southbank program in 2013 and The Writers' Studio (TWS) in 2015. KT can be found online at www.northernlightsgothic.com and @KT_Wagner on Twitter.

Zoey Xolton

Zoey Xolton dreams darkly and often. Over the years these dreams have come to shape her waking reality, and so it has eventuated that she lives out her days on this earth as a Storyteller. Her tales are often filled with the paranormal and fantastical, tempered with lashings of forbidden romance and always driven home with a strong element of tragedy! When she's not writing, Zoey can be found chasing after her precocious children and swooning over her own dark prince—the man she is lucky enough to call her husband and best friend. You can find out more about Zoey and her works at her website: www.zoeyxolton.com.

SNEAK PREVIEW OF
THE JOY THIEF
(CATHELL SERIES BOOK 3)

A.M. Rycroft

EXCERPT

Theo faded into the crowd with practiced ease. Aeryn watched her go with a mixture of awe at the young thief's skill and apprehension that Theo might get herself into trouble on her own. She turned away, reminding herself that she was not Theo's parent and had no right to stifle her independence. Theo had had no one but herself to rely on long before she and Aeryn met. It was no wonder she felt chafed by Aeryn's constant presence.

Aeryn walked off in the opposite direction through the market's main thoroughfare. She stopped at a fruit vendor and picked through the selection in the woman's display, putting aside a few pieces. As she reached forward to snag a pouch of dried fruit for Theo, a sudden prickling sensation touched the back of her neck, a warning that someone was watching her.

She waited a moment to see if it passed, acting as though she did not even notice it. The sensation only grew. Aeryn straightened and slowly turned her head to glance around the marketplace.

Her watcher, a man dressed in black robes, was not hard to find. He stood by the corner of a building diagonal to the cart. He openly stared at her, and his gaze possessed the intensity of someone who wanted her to know he was watching.

Nothing about him was familiar. The lines of tattoos down both sides and across the base of his neck would make him hard to forget. From where she stood, she could not make out whether the tattoos were words or symbols. The watcher appeared human; he was broad shouldered and slightly overweight. His sleeves were pushed back to reveal well-muscled forearms, which were crossed over his chest.

Their eyes locked across the distance between them. The man did not look away or even blink. He simply continued to stare at her. She sensed conflict in his gaze, malice toward her mixed with something else. A clear sense of warning settled into her gut as they continued to stare across the market at each other.

She made up her mind to confront him, to find out who he was and what he wanted, but a sharp exclamation next to her stole her attention.

"It's wickedness, I tell you!"

Aeryn shot a glance in the direction of the old woman who had cried out. She was talking to an adjacent vendor. When Aeryn turned her gaze back to the black-robed man, she found he was gone. She searched for him but could not see him at the other vendor stalls or at either end of the street. It was as if he had simply vanished.

She glanced back at the old woman and the vendor again.

"The boy'll be fine," the vendor was saying.

The old woman shook her head. "I'm tellin' you, Jonan, there was nothin' wrong with him. Then, all of a sudden, he comes up sick. It's some kind of wickedness that's happened to him and the others."

"Don' be superstitious, Mabe. Boys get sick. They eat something that don't agree with 'em, or they just catch the vapors from being outside when the fog's in and too thick. Nothin' wicked about it."

The woman shook her head. "It's nothin' like the vapors or eatin' something he shouldn't have. He barely moves or speaks. Mind you, I ain't seen him for myself, but that's what Hamish told me last night. He says when the boy looks at you, he looks *haunted*." Mabe shuddered dramatically. "The neighbor's boy ain't the first one neither, and you know it. You've heard people talkin'."

"Aye. I've heard the stories. I don't believe 'em. Nothing but a coincidence."

"You're bein' a fool, Jonan," the woman muttered. "Ignorin' it don't make it go away. We have to face up to the evil that's been happenin' to our young'uns and ask the High Mother to save them." The old woman traced a star shape on her chest with her finger.

Jonan frowned deeply, but he seemed to be out of arguments to give her. Both he and Mabe fell silent. The old woman, still agitated, shook her head and then held up two small loaves of bread to indicate what she was taking. After she paid Jonan, she stalked off down the street, the bread cradled in her arms.

His eyes met Aeryn's. He shook his head. "Don't mind her ravings. She's old and superstitious. She sees boogeymen everywhere."

Aeryn nodded and turned her attention back to the fruit vendor. She smiled weakly at Aeryn, perhaps concerned that the old woman's outburst might make her rethink buying the fruit she had set aside. Aeryn smiled back, though her mind was now troubled. She paid for the dried fruit and other items, which the vendor dropped in a sack for her, and then turned away from the vendors' carts.

Between the appearance of the black-robed man and the old woman's outburst, Aeryn began to wonder if Eben had been her best choice for a place to stop overnight. Regardless of what Jonan said, the old woman's story made her think back to the city watchman at Eben's gates, the one who had stared at Theo. The sadness in his eyes had been unmistakable.

What was it he had been thinking about? What did it have to do with Theo?

A knot of tension formed inside her. Rabid

dogs. Black-robed men. Mysterious illnesses. She felt the stab of a headache coming on. She raised her fingertips to her forehead, rubbing it, and tracing over the thin white scar that split her left eyebrow. She had hoped their troubles were over when they left Pius and the taint of The Harbinger behind.

Aeryn looked down at the packages of supplies tucked under her arm. She decided what she had purchased would have to be enough. She adjusted Aric, slung across her back, and then turned in the direction Theo had gone. As much as she wanted Theo to have her independence, it was time for her to find the young thief before something else found her first.

The Joy Thief
Coming April 2017

To find out more about this series and subscribe to new release alert emails, visit our website at www.mightyquillbooks.com.

6 | The Joy Thief